the placebo effect trilogy

like blood in water

the future of giraffes

view of delft

What unites the three collections that make up *The Placebo Effect Trilogy* into a single novel-like structure are the themes that like motifs in music are repeated throughout them, binding them together the way characters and events in a traditional trilogy bind three separate novels into a unified work. In this the trilogy is like a complex musical composition, a symphony in three movements—a symphony of semantics rather than of sound. The unity of the work is further heightened by the form common to the three books—each of them consists of five *mininovels* which employ *negative text*—missing information the reader has to provide himself—that imparts the scope of novels to these short-story-sized texts.

The subject of the trilogy is life—the placebo effect of the empty sugar-coated pill of faith in the future encoded in the genes of every human being.

Like Blood in Water introduces the main themes which recur in the two subsequent books. These are alienation (all of the five mininovels, but in particular "Former Pianist Fitipaldo), the scream as a manifestation of existential despair ("Screaming," "Pavarotti-Agamemnon"), loss of a child ("Screaming," "The Joys and Sorrows of R. York," "Pavarotti-Agamemnon"), and the fear of death (all five works).

The unifying topic in *The Future of Giraffes* is childhood. It is the subject of all five mininovels in the book. The first of them, "A Day in the Life," picks up the theme of screaming from the first book and introduces the theme of abandonment, a variant of the loss of a child, which reappears in the remaining four works, most vividly in the fourth mininovel, "The Quarry." The second mininovel, "The Short Unhappy Life of Pinky Schmuck," introduces the theme of departure from the norm (cognitive impairment) which is repeated in the third work, "Your Childhood," where it is presented in the form of albinism. The fifth mininovel, "Sunday Morning," whose main topic is abandonment, serves as the companion book-end to the first mininovel, the action in it taking place in physical surroundings substantially similar to those in the first.

All of the works in *View of Delft* contain German elements—characters, language, physical surroundings, textual allusions, and so forth—a theme introduced in the second book in "The Short Unhappy Life of Pinky Schmuck" and "Your Childhood." The themes of alienation and cognitive impairment are picked up in "The Idiot," the first work in the book. The subject of alienation is further treated in the next two mininovels, "Years of Travel" and "The Albino Syndrome." This latter work, as the title states, picks up the theme of albinism introduced in the second book which is a symbolic representation of the fear of death. (The fact that the same character appears in the two works further strengthens the unity of the trilogy.) The topic of death is treated in the last three mininovels, "The Albino Syndrome," "Karla and Georg or the Ambiguous Nature of Clouds," and in particular "The School," where it is the main subject. The principal character in this work is named Rohark, which alludes to the principal character in the first work in *Like Blood in Water*, Roark, the two mininovels thus acting as book-ends to the trilogy. Both of these names, of course, have the word "roar' embedded in them, which is an emphatic equivalent of the word "scream."

yuriy tarnawsky

yuriy tarnawsky

the future of giraffes
five mininovels

Journal of Experimental Fiction 53.2

JEF Books/Journal of Experimental Fiction/Depth Charge

Geneva, Illinois

The Placebo Effect Trilogy (ltd. edition boxed set)

ISBN 1-884097-53-7/ISBN-13 978-1-884097-53-9

Also published as *Journal of Experimental Fiction* 53

ISSN 1084-547X

Individual Volumes:

like blood in water

ISBN 1-884097-25-1/ISBN-13 978-1-884097-25-6

the future of giraffes

ISBN 1-884097-26-X/ISBN-13 978-1-884097-26-3

view of delft

ISBN 1-884097-27-8/ISBN-13 978-1-884097-27-0

Front Cover Art and Design: Norman Conquest

Book Design: Eckhard Gerdes

Typefaces: Goudy Old Style (body), PicturePostcard (headers)

Produced and Printed in the United States of America

The foremost in innovative fiction

http://experimentalfiction.com

the future of giraffes

five mininovels

For my daughter Ustya,
so that she'd understand

table of contents

a day in the life

I. cold

The door opens and a woman comes in. The boy raises himself up on his left elbow without pushing away the covers and looks.

She is middle-aged, tall and thin, with a bony masculine face, long-nosed and flat-cheeked, and wears a gray frock with a round white collar and a full-length white apron over it. Her head is tied in a white kerchief and wisps of straight gray hair stick out from under it in places.

The woman carries in front of her a big white enameled washbasin, from the way she moves and it moves in her hands, appearing to be filled full with water. Over her left shoulder she carries a white linen towel neatly folded into a narrow strip.

She stops, carefully closes the door with her right foot behind her (it opens counterclockwise into the room), and steps forward. Her movements and that of the basin don't change, confirming the latter is filled close to the brim.

There is one window in the room, small and square, with a small square table under it of the same size as if its opaque image, and the woman comes up to it, puts the basin down, and lays the towel next to it on the right leaving it partly draped over the edge of the table.

The window is wide open with both of its sides in. Outside lies a small-town landscape with rolling hills, close up overgrown with trees among which can be seen mostly single-storied houses, and farther in the distance bigger treeless ones covered with what looks like tall yellow grass. The hills show off exuberantly their shapes like whales frolicking in the sea, jumping out of the water and plunging gracefully back into it. It is a clear summer morning with a pristine blue sky and crispness in the air that has a sting to it like rubbing alcohol on freshly shaven skin.

The woman turns around to face the boy and says in a clear, loud voice, It's getting late. Get up. You have a long day before you.

There is a stern expression on her face as she looks at the boy but interest shows through it like original text through the new one in a palimpsest.

The boy doesn't stir for a few seconds trying to savor the warmth collected under the comforter just a little longer but then throws the covers off with one quick moment of his right arm and jumps out of bed.

He wears a loose white knee-length night shirt and feels the cold air rush under it from below moving eagerly upward, making sure it doesn't miss any exposed spot on his body, trying to assert itself over it. The bare floor is hard and also cold under his feet.

The boy walks quickly toward the window where the basin sits on the table and the woman moves aside to make room for him.

Once she has stirred she doesn't stop but continues walking toward the door, comes up to it, opens it, and gets ready to walk out.

She stops unexpectedly however and turning to the boy as before calmly says, Rub yourself well with the water as you wash. It'll do you good.

But don't splash too much, she ads. And wipe up the water when you finish. The last time you left it wet.

With what? The boy asks loudly, ignoring her last remark, not turning his face to her as if not caring how she might answer.

With your shirt, the woman replies again calmly, turns away, walks out, and closes the door. You can hear her footsteps getting softer behind it.

The boy pulls the shirt off his body with one quick movement as he had thrown off the covers, tosses it on the floor, and stands still, looking out the window, unaware of it huddling against his left foot, covering its toes as if wanting to keep them warm.

He is stark naked. The cold streaming in through the window is like the sharp point of a knife pressed deep into his flesh just before breaking the skin.

He has seen the view many times before and has stopped paying attention to it but this time watches it wih great interest. He is aware of this and doesn't know why but then realizes it is because he understands for the first time that there is no connection between the landscape and him. Whatever happens to it has no bearing on him and the other way around. He finds this remarkable and concludes it is an important discovery. He feels it is a memorable event in his life, part of his growing up, and that he will never forget it.

He remembers the water in the basin. With one more quick movement like the two preceding ones he bends down, sticks his hands in the water, scoops some of it up, and throws it over his face.

It is ice cold.

The boy makes a sound halfway between a scream of pain and a laugh, sticks his hands in the water again, scoops some of it up once more, and throws it over his chest, rubbing it hard into his skin. Its coldness has the roughness of sandpaper.

He proceeds washing himself in this fashion, from time to time making sounds like the first one, throwing water over various parts of his body and rubbing it hard into his skin as if shaping it with the cold for what will come.

2. bread and water

A room with tall bare walls and one small square window tightly shut. Pale morning sunlight in it like limp cobwebs. A long bare rectangular wooden table with a stool at one of its corners. The boy sitting on the latter at one of the narrower ends of the table facing it, his knees tightly pressed together, his hands dutifully resting on his lap.

The door opens and the woman from the preceding scene comes in. She is dressed as before and this time carries a small aluminum cup in her left hand and a matching aluminum plate with a thick wedge of dark bread cut from a big loaf in the right one. Both the cup and the plate are dented in places. The cup seems to be filled to the brim with liquid because the woman caries it carefully making sure the liquid doesn't spill.

The woman shuts the door with her right foot as she had done in the boy's room, comes up to the table, and puts the two things down in front of the boy. Having done this she steps a few feet to the side and stands there with her arms folded on her chest watching the boy with interest.

It is clear now the cup is filled with water.

The woman has put the cup on the right side of the plate. The boy picks it up carefully with his right hand, moves it to the other side, picks it up with his left hand, and drinks from it. He then puts it down, picks up the piece of bread with his right hand, brings it to his lips, bites into it, and chews.

After chewing a few times he picks up the cup once again with his left hand, drinks from it, puts it down, bites into the piece of bread again, and proceeds chewing on it.

He eats like this from then on with the woman watching him attentively in silence and without stirring.

The boy has eaten almost all of the bread and drunk up nearly all of the water and continues eating.

Do you want more? The woman asks.

The boy makes a two-syllable sound with his mouth closed (he is chewing on the bread) and nods in the affirmative.

He swallows what he has chewed up, picks up the cup, drinks from it, emptying it completely, puts it down on the table, pushes it in the woman's direction, and then does the same with the plate. He puts the rest of the bread which he holds in his right hand in his mouth and goes on chewing on it.

The woman steps up to the table, picks up the cup and the plate, and prepares to take them away.

She turns partly toward the door but at the last minute stops and asks, Do you want water too?

The boy makes a sound like the preceding one and nods in the affirmative. He then swallows quickly what he has in his mouth and says, Yes.

You can tell from his voice there is still some food in his mouth.

The boy swallows again this time more slowly and then once more quickly as before .

The woman turns toward the door, comes up to it, opens it, and walks out, shutting it behind her.

Once more you can hear her footsteps getting softer as she walks away.

3. furniture

You still have a little time to spare, so go and take a nap, the woman says to the boy and he goes into his room, lies down on the bed, turns right toward the wall, and goes to sleep.

Immediately he has the following dream.

He hears the door open, so he rolls over to his left and sees the woman come in as she had done earlier.

Get up, she says. We have to move the furniture out.

Obediently he gets up, she comes up to the bed, and they both lift it up and carry it to the door. It is a bunk bed as in reality but lighter than he remembers it being, which surprises him, and they have no difficulty carrying it.

She has left the door open and they carry the bed out through it again without any difficulty.

There is a huge dark room on the other side of the door where furniture has been stacked up helter-skelter against the wall on the right. The rest of the house must have been emptied of the furniture already.

They bring the bed to where the furniture is, stand it up on one of its narrow sides, and tip it over so that it rests at an angle. The bedclothes and the mattress slip off the bed in the process and lie in a heap on the floor partly held down by the end of the bed.

After they do this the woman heads back to the door without saying anything and he obediently follows her. She said earlier they have to move the furniture out.

On coming into the room the woman comes up to the table under the window and stands next to it.

He comes up to its other end, they lift the table up, carry it into the next room, and dump it onto the pile of furniture next to the bed in the same way they have done with the latter, in other words standing it on one of its sides and tipping it over.

Next they tackle the chest of drawers that stands against the wall on the left of the door. They don't try lifting it up but push it on the floor, the woman doing most of the pushing on one of its narrow sides and he on the wide one on her left, helping her push and making sure the chest moves in the right direction.

Having pushed the chest to where the furniture is they start pulling the drawers out of it. They are empty, and at first he is surprised at this but then accepts it as normal. Given the situation they couldn't be full.

They throw the drawers on top of the furniture making sure they don't come down and then tip the chest over onto the pile taking care it stays in place as they have done with the bed and the table.

He remembers there is still the chair left in the room and thinks he should get it, so he says he'll do it to the woman, but she replies she will get it herself and he should wait.

He keeps his eyes on her until she disappears through the door and then turns left to look at the furniture.

There is a huge pile of it reaching almost to the ceiling but he can see light shining through it from the other side.

He peers in closer through the gaps in the furniture and sees there is a hole in the wall behind it—actually not a hole but a wide opening. A good part of the wall in that spot is gone. It has been knocked down as part of what piling up of the furniture is about.

He continues looking through the hole and sees beyond it the familiar landscape of houses hidden among trees up close and rolling hills in the distance.

A feeling of some kind starts forming itself in him but at that instant he hears the woman coming back and he stops it from developing further and turns to face her.

She is carrying in her hands a small white plate with an apple and a knife on top of it. She gives it to him without saying anything, turns away, and walks in the direction of the kitchen. She seems to have forgotten about the chair.

He remembers the chair but doesn't find anything strange in the woman's behavior and turns his attention to the apple.

He knows he is supposed to eat it but doesn't know how. It is clear he should use the knife on it but how can he do it when there is nothing for him to put the plate on? He can't do it while holding on to the plate.

Perplexed, he stands staring at the apple and the knife, not knowing what to do. The idea he could put the plate on the floor doesn't enter his mind.

4. apples

The boy lies for a while with his eyes open and then realizes he is awake and remembers the apple in the dream.

Immediately he recalls lying at night in his parent's bedroom in the special bed they kept there when he was little and not feeling well, hearing through the open window apples in the orchard outside falling from the trees to the ground, sounding like oboes playing long soft sounds. He would fall asleep listening to them and they would play for him all through the night until the bright morning.

Energized, he jumps out of bed, runs to the window, gets on top of the tale, jumps outside, and runs around the corner into the orchard.

He runs in among the trees, throws his head back, and looks up. Each tree has apples orbiting it like many planets helter-skelter a sun. The sight is beautiful. He is surprised he has never noticed it before.

A tree attracts his attention. He runs up to it, climbs up its trunk, stands up on one of its big branches, climbs higher, then still higher, sees a beautiful red apple hanging on a branch nearby, climbs still a little higher, reaches out with his hand for it, it is too far, he leans farther out, stretches his hand out again, strains, opens his fingers, and finally touches it. It sways gently, trying to elude him, but finally gives in and he grasps its round hard form.

It is like a girl's breast under the blouse felt by a man's hand as he recalls being described in a book he has read recently. He plucks it, makes himself comfortable standing on the branch and leaning against the trunk, rubs it in his fingers, brings it to his lips, and bites into it. Its juice bursts forth into his mouth and its taste spreads through his consciousness. It is sweet and tart at the same time and delicious. He closes his eyes from the sensation like a cat in warm sunshine, chews on the chunk he has bitten off, and swallows it. He proceeds eating the apple in this fashion, safe in his spot, his feet steady on the branch and his back pressed against the trunk.

He gets used to the taste of the apple and after a while looks around. He sees straight ahead the white walls and the red roof of his house through the gaps among the trees and the open space of he road running past the orchard along the river on the left. He strains to see if he might spot the light shapes of the children from the nearby orphanage in their gray uniforms walking in pairs in a file with the two nuns behind them along the road but there aren't any. It is too late for that. They go to the mass early and must be already back from church. He followed them once to the orphanage and saw them recite something standing obediently in rows facing one of the nuns and then sing, watching furtively through the closed window holding his breath and with his heart pounding while huddling against the wall.

Suddenly his thinking is interrupted. They are calling for him to come. He has to climb down.

5. a game of chess

Dark tree-covered mountains stretching as far as the eye can see in all directions like the sound of cannons far away. The sky overhead a uniform deep blue. Not a cloud in it. On the ground all around tall yellow grass like a cool fire. The sunshine blinding but the air bracing like the feel of toilet water drying on the skin.

The boy lies on a blanket on his left side watching his father and another man play chess, the chessboard between them. The father on the blanket next to him also on his left side raised on his elbow, his broad back under a white shirt blocking much of the view, his legs in light gray pants stretched out, his shiny black shoes sticking out of them daubed with blotches of white light as if splashed with white paint. The suit jacket he wore draped over his shoulders as they walked along the hills to the spot neatly folded on the edge of the blanket higher up.

The man lies in a mirror-image position on his right side, his body also supported on his elbow. He wears a likewise white shirt with a checkered black and white tie and pants of a darker shade of gray and black shoes. His black hair shiny with brilliantine is parted on the left and neatly combed over his skull, its natural waves largely successfully breaking through. He wears a black pencil-thin moustache and small round black-rimmed glasses.

Beyond the man on another blanket a little higher up the boy's mother sits with her feet pointing in the same direction as those of the men and her knees drawn up and pressed together. She wears a loose white blouse with long sleeves and a round collar and a dark gray skirt that reaches down to the middle of her calves. Her shoes are not visible. She has long wavy dark brown hair tied loosely in the back and wears a gold-framed pince-nez on her nose. Next to her on her left sits the man's wife, her image almost fully blocked by the boy's mother. She is dressed in something dark.

A basket with a tall arched handle sits on top of a white square tablecloth in the grass behind the boy's mother, the neck of a big clear glass seltzer water bottle with a white porcelain stopper and a red rubber ring attached to it sticking out. Some plates and containers with food can be seen carelessly distributed on the tablecloth around the basket.

The mother and the woman are talking in soft voices with each other. Sounds of the voices of more than two children shouting and laughing coming from higher up on the left spreading in the air.

The sound of a chess piece is heard being put down hard on the board. It is the boy's father making a move.

I heard the other day on the radio that herds of giraffes have been seen lately in Africa fleeing from something, the man says calmly. And it's not just in one place.... All over the region.... Running from the east to the west.

A much softer sound of a piece being put down on the board is heard next. The man has made a move in response to that of the boy's father.

They must be fleeing some calamity, the boy's father says calmly. There's been a bad drought there for years so it's probably fires in the savannahs.

Check, he says as he puts down a piece hard on the board.

There is silence for a few seconds.

In one town a giraffe strayed away from the herd and ran through the town, the man says. The traffic policeman motioned for it to stop and it did... like a car.... And then it moved again when he motioned for it to go.

He moves a piece but you can barely hear the sound it makes as it is put down on the board.

Check, the boy's father says coldly as if not having heard the man's words, putting the piece down hard on the board.

Maybe it was a tame one, he ads after a white, One that escaped from a circus.

The boy would like to put his hand on his father's back and feel its warmth and strength through the shirt as he had done many times before but feels too lazy to do it. He rolls over onto his back, shuts his eyes, and drifts off into sleep, no longer paying attention to the voices, hearing only the sounds of the chess pieces being put down on the board like someone's determined footsteps on a hard floor growing fainter and fainter, moving farther and farther away.

The last thing he remembers is someone covering him with something light and kissing him gently on the eyes. He knows it is his mother.

6. giraffes

He dreams he is in a herd of giraffes galloping wildly, riding one of them, clinging desperately to its neck. Its back is sharp down the middle so that it hurts his crotch and rises steeply toward the neck and he has to make sure he doesn't slip off and fall to the ground.

The animals are like sea waves rising and falling all around him. The sky is low, brown like the flat earth he can see on the sides and up ahead, and only a small strip of red and yellow light on the horizon illuminates it up ahead on the left. This must be where the sun is setting.

His parents and sister are with him riding giraffes too—the father a few animals up ahead and the sister and mother on separate animals on the left.

The giraffes gallop like horses, their necks leaning forward and their eyes (those of the few he can see) bulging like those of animals being slaughtered.

They must be fleeing a fire because the hair on the backs of the necks of some of them is burning. Sparks fly off the animals' necks like those off the roofs of houses burning in a strong wind. The necks burn with red and yellow flames similar to the light on the horizon as if related to it.

They gallop on and on and it doesn't seem they will ever stop. He feels safe however because of being with his family and his father leading the way. The sound of the animals' hoofs on the ground is soothing like that of one's heartbeat.

Suddenly things change. He is no longer in a herd but alone on top of his giraffe.

It is much darker all around now and quiet as if in an empty city street at night. It seems his giraffe has strayed off from the herd into a town they were passing. It doesn't seem to have noticed it however because it is galloping calmly as before.

But suddenly again it seems to notice what it has done because it starts running faster and unevenly, as if upset, jumping up and down, which makes it harder for him to stay on its back. He nearly slips off a few times.

He clings to the giraffe's neck with all his might but it is too wide for him to put his arms around it and its short hair is slippery and his hands keep slipping off it.

He grabs the hair on the giraffe's neck but it is too short and too stiff for him to hold onto.

The giraffe's gallop is reminiscent now of a cart going over uneven cobblestones—the animal shakes so violently he can't even hold his hands on its neck. He presses his legs together to keep himself from sliding off but it is useless. He starts tipping over to his left, keeps on sliding down, and eventually falls to the ground.

He hits the ground hard but doesn't seem to be hurt and sees the giraffe gallop off down the middle of the street and disappear in the near darkness.

Slowly he raises himself, stands up and looks around.

The street is bathed in gray light as if everything were covered with ashes.

The houses are all low, mostly one- and sometime two-storied, with flat facades and roofs such as he has seen in pictures of African countries. All the windows in them are black as if empty and so are the doors.

He looks closer and sees it is true—the houses are all empty, with the glass in the windows gone and doors missing from their hinges, and seem to have been abandoned for a long time.

Fear overcomes him. Could it be that the town is deserted?

He doesn't want to believe it and runs down the street calling out, Hello! and, Is there anyone there? But no one replies. The houses he passes are all empty like the ones before.

He runs on and on, calling out constantly, his voice growing more and more desperate, but knows it is in vain. The town is empty and there is no one to help him.

Finally he stops, panting wildly, trying to catch his breath He can feel himself growing numb and the hair on top of his head stirring, trying to stand up. He is in a ghost town in the middle of the desert all alone!

7. alone

It is the emptiness of the sky that makes him realize he is awake. He lies on his back with his eyes open. For an instant he expects to feel that fear of falling into it and disappearing that comes over him each time he stares into it when it is clear and blue but realizes it is not the same as it had been when he was awake. It is still cloudless but with a trace of gray in it as from the sun being low in the sky. It seems to have gotten late in the day.

A different fear now seizes his heart. Has he slept that long? He only had one dream and it seemed short. How could it be?

Before he has had time to address this question he realizes it is perfectly still all around and that there is emptiness on his left where his father had sat. The latter is no longer there.

He quickly sits up and sees he is alone. His parents, sister, the couple they were with, and their children are all gone. Gone are also the blankets they had sat on, the chessboard, and the basket they had brought the food in. The blanket he slept on is still under him but the spread his mother covered him with as he was falling asleep is also gone.

His heart sinks and pounds loudly. What has happened? He jumps up and looks around.

There is no one anywhere as far as he can see.

Are they playing a joke on him, hiding in the grass, trying to scare him because he has slept so long? That would be nasty of them.

He yells, Mom! Dad!, angry inside and runs around in a big circle through the tall grass but there is no trace of anyone anywhere. Everyone is definitely gone.

What could have happened? He asks himself. Where have they all gone to? Why did they leave him behind? Was it because it had gotten late and it was time to leave but he was sleeping so soundly and they didn't want to wake him up?

The explanation doesn't make sense. You don't do something like this to a child, especially your own. His parents wouldn't have left him behind on their own. Something must have forced them to do it. But what?

His mind cannot come up with an answer.

He stops thinking, runs around through the grass in a still bigger circle calling for his parents and looking as far as he can in all directions but sees no one and in the end stops. He mind goes back to his explanation. It must be true. It had gotten late and they had to leave but he looked tired and slept soundly so they decided not to wake him up but go by themselves. He would realize what had happened and would go home once he woke up.

A thought flashes through his mind that if this were true they would have left him covered with the spread, for him to stay worm, but he immediately counters it with the answer that they might have thought that the spread and the blanket would have been too much for him to carry and so they took the former with them. After all it clearly wasn't needed because he didn't feel cold sleeping without it. Another thought then flashes through his mind that he may have thrown the spread off by himself because of feeling hot and so there was no reason for them to leave it behind.

Yes, that must have been the case for sure, he concludes with joy and decides to run home. Everyone will be waiting for him when he gets there and everything will be as it has always been!

Elated he starts running in the direction of town but after a few steps realizes he has left the blanket on the ground and so he turns back, picks it up, gathers it up into a loose bundle, and pressing it to his chest runs in his former direction, the image of his being home with his family vivid in his mind.

His worries haven't left him however and they keep coming back to him over and over as he runs, forcing their way back each time he suppresses them like a rock chafing the foot, moving around in one's shoe. His parents wouldn't have left him behind of their own volition. Something unusual must have made them do it. It couldn't possibly have been something benign.

He makes his way along the hill down into a valley, and then up to the top of another hill, and as he crests it he sees the town spread out before him along the river with its dense green trees, the white walls and red roofs of its houses, and the church spires sticking up sharp into the sky here and there.

He can't see his house from the spot but knows where it is and this once again makes him feel better. Soon he will be home, the mystery of his having been left behind will be resolved, and his life will go back to normal.

Exhausted though that he is and out of breath he pushes on, pressing the blanket to his chest and keeping his eyes on the spot where his house stands as if afraid it would disappear if he let it out of sight.

He decides not to follow the usual road home but to take a shortcut through the fields and backyards so as to be there sooner.

8. alone

He climbs over the fence and finally is in the orchard in the back of his house. It stands there up ahead as always big and solid and he can see its outline through the trees.

He doesn't let the memory of his being there earlier that day come up to the surface but runs on, finds himself out in the open, and stops. His heart sinks.

The windows in the house are all wide open which he has never seen before.

Something bad must have happened!

He rushes madly around the corner to the front of the house and sees the same is true there.

The gate in the fence is wide open too as is the front door.

Clutching the blanket to his chest with all his might, his heart beating wildly, he runs into the house and sees that the hallway is empty. All the furniture has been taken out of it.

His heart is up in his throat. He can't find an explanation for what he sees but abandons the effort and runs into the living room hoping everything will be alright there. It is empty however the same as the hallway. All the furniture has also been taken out of it.

Mom! Dad! He yells at the top of his voice looking around in despair but there is no answer. The stillness and emptiness is like a huge rock he can't make disappear. The unblocked view of the outside through the wide open windows makes the room seem emptier too. It is as if its space ceased being part of the house and joined the vast outside.

He remembers the dream he had earlier that day before setting out on the hike with his family, the hole in the wall he saw through the piled up furniture and the feeling that had started to form itself in him as he looked through it which he didn't let fully unfold. It was going to be the same he has at this moment.

He knows now how things will turn out.

He tries to deny it and like a gadfly gone crazy in a closed space runs madly through the house yelling, Mom! and, Dad!, hoping he will be wrong but finds his suspicion confirmed again and again. There are little things like a sock, other items of clothing, kitchen utensils, and so on lying on the floor here and there. In one corner he spots a little wooden horse which was a favorite toy of his when he was little lying on its side. It had gotten lost somewhere and he had been looking for it for a long time and couldn't find it and now it is here. He could take it. But it is of no value to him now and he runs on. Otherwise the house is all empty. Every stick of furniture has been taken out it and everyone is gone.

Still hoping to refute this he runs outside, stops, and this time yells, Dad! over and over again but there is no reply.

He turns around toward the house and sees its roof dark against the still bright sky. It seems to have grown darker and taller.

This worries him for an instant but he dismisses the feeling. The real problem is something else. His family is all gone and he doesn't know what has happened to them. He fears he never see them again.

He recalls wanting to touch his father's back as he was falling asleep and being too lazy to do it. He wishes he had done it. At least he would have had one more memory of him if he is gone forever.

But he realizes that this wouldn't have mattered. One more little memory wouldn't have made any difference. What he needs is his father alive with him.

A thought flashes through his mind that he is being punished for having been too lazy then to touch his father's back but he dismisses it immediately. It is too silly to think something like that. No one is ever punished in such a terrible way for something as small as this. This is especially true for a child.

He pushes these thoughts out of his mind, turns around again, and runs toward the gate.

Under the bush next to it he sees the chair from his room lying on its side. One of its legs is missing. It got broken as it was being taken away and was left behind.

He notices then he no longer carries the blanket. He dropped it somewhere as he was running through the house.

He thinks of running back inside and looking for it but decides against it. His having lost his blanket is not important. Once again the real problem is his family being gone.

He thinks of their neighbors. They should be able to tell him what has happened to his parents and home.

He runs into their yard and stops.

The windows in their house are all wide open too. The place looks empty. Next to the wall in one spot there is a heap of broken furniture.

Their house has also been ransacked and they are gone!

He doesn't understand it. What could have happened? What does all this mean? He is desperate.

He runs back to his house and then out into the street.

It is empty. The river runs along it and there is a street on its other side which is normally busy.

The river is narrow in this spot and you can see well the other street from where he stands. It is all quiet with no traffic or other sign of life in it this time however. The whole town has been deserted and he's been left alone!

He grows numb at the thought and feels the hair on his head stir trying to stand up as it had done in the dream.

He wants to call out to someone for help but can think of no name so he yells as hard as he thinks he can, Aaaaaaaaa! bending down in the knees to make it easier for himself.

Immediately he realizes he can scream harder however and so he pushes his voice more and more until it can't get any louder.

He holds it at this level continuing to scream but eventually realizes it is in vain for no matter how hard he screamed it would never be loud enough.

the short unhappy life

of pinky schmuck

I. pinky is born

It's time to get going Pinky, his mother said firmly in her hoarse masculine voice and slapped her bare belly with the palm of her hand. And then she gave it a real hard whack with the edge of her clenched fist for good measure.

Pinky sloshed around in the amniotic fluid inside her as if romping around in starched freshly ironed bed sheets for a while but realized he couldn't delay the inevitable act any longer and had to obey his mother's order. She was not one to fool around with.

Outside it was a gloomy late late fall morning with gray mist hanging in the cold air, the smell of rotting leaves delicious like that of the choicest of Havana cigars trying to mingle with it helped out in its endeavor by a barely detectable scent of distant smoke. They were burning leaves somewhere in spite of it being wet and against the strict town- as well as country-wide injunction.

His father was nowhere to be seen (at that instant and for the rest of their, that is Pinky's as well as his own, lives) and out in the yard a red wheel barrow stood alone next to a dilapidated wood shed with a rusty corrugated roof and plain wooden board walls once pained a brilliant hopeful white. Three or four ducks waddled aimlessly around it like round objects rolling from side to side in a box being transported in a vehicle moving at breakneck speed along a winding country road. Beyond the shed a likewise once painted a brilliant hopeful white picket fence like a drunk was trying to stand up in a few places but had given up and lay prostrate in the tall unruly grass in all the other. The landscape on the other side of it was lost for good in the mist.

A tall white coffee cup stained brown along the edges stood on the table under the window in the kitchen with cold black coffee on its bottom staring out like a hostile eye. To the right high up on the white-tiled wall the electric clock had stopped at 4:07. Below it water dripped from the faucet at precisely one drop per second feeling obliged to help out in the situation.

2. martha

Inside behind the screen door hanging limply on one hinge like an injured bird's wing all was topsy-turvy as behind his back in the yard. The kitchen table sagged on one side where its leg was missing like a tent with one of its poles removed. Two of the three chairs lay broken on their sides looking like teeth knocked out in a vicious fight. (They were white.) The third one leaned with its back against the cabinet with the sink in it resting on one leg like an acrobat balancing himself on one arm in an impossibly difficult position. Dishes had been scooped up from the sink and scattered smashed all over the floor. Those in the cabinets on the wall above have been swept out and made to join the other ones in the same fashion. The clock on the wall with its permanently frozen time had been left untouched however as had been the faucet below it and water continued dripping from it calmly at an even pace indifferent to, as if oblivious of the devastation all around.

The inside of the house gaped black like a bottomless horizontal pit in the opening of the door leading into the next room.

Pinky teetered forward on his short stiff legs like a toy wardrobe tilting from side to side trying to move on its own, his arms outstretched, his fingers curved desperately like a bird's claws ready to grasp anything that might come their way, their fingernails trying to help out anyway they could, eyes full of tears, cheeks streaming with them, mouth wide open, a tiny black chasm inside it trying in vain to match the huge one ahead, screaming at the top of his voice, Martha! Marthaaaaaa!, tears from his cheeks inexplicably flying in the direction of his voice in a futile attempt to help it.

3. dirt and worms

The schoolyard of Pinky's school after classes. A dark gloomy afternoon with thick dark clouds hanging over the earth like branches of a monstrously big and dense chestnut tree. The yard in addition shaded by a real giant and dense chestnut tree extending over nearly all of it. The yard therefore unnaturally dark. The air cold and damp from recent rains. The ground bare and also damp from recent rains. It is dark and soft all over and fluffy in places.

Pinky standing with his back pressed against the huge tree trunk as if against a shut door. Three boys, his classmates, of the same age as he but taller and stronger gathered around him. The outside two holding his arms against the tree pressing down hard on them. The middle one with Pinky's shirt crumpled up into a tight ball in his fist pressing down even harder on the latter's chest. The boy's face close to Pinky's. Pinky staring with unfocused eyes at his chief tormentor like a farsighted person unable to see something close up.

The boy in the middle (*with profound hatred*): Your mother called you Schmuck because you're a prick.

Pinky *(desperate):* No she didn't. She gave me my father's name and it means jewel.

The boy in the middle: No it doesn't. It means prick.

Pinky: No it means jewel in German. My father's German.

The boy in the middle *(with contempt):* You don't have a father. You're a bastard.

Pinky *(more desperate):* Yes I do. My father lives in Germany... in a castle on the Rhine. He's a nobleman. That's why his name is Jewel.

The boy in the middle: No he isn't. He's also a prick. That's why they called him Schmuck.

Pinky *(emphatic):* No they didn't. It's his family's name. It means jewel in German.

The boy in the middle: No it doesn't. It means prick.

Pinky *(more emphatic):* It means prick in Yiddish. In German it means jewel.

The boy in the middle (*with greater contempt than before*): You're not German. You're a Jew!

Pinky (*once again desperate*): No I'm not. I'm German.

The boy in the middle: You're a tike! (*He hasn't mastered the phonetics of the intended word.*)

Pinky (*yelps like a puppy someone has stepped on*): I'm not! I'm German! I'm not a tike. (*He has never heard the intended or the uttered word before and doesn't know the meaning of either of them.*)

The boy in the middle (*with profound contempt*): You're a dirty Jew!

Pinky (*crying desperately*): I'm not! I'm a clean German!

The boy in the middle (*pulling Pinky down to the ground with the other two boys' help*): You're not. You're a dirty Jew.... You're a schmuck! (*He grabs Pinky's hair with his hand and turns his head face down. Presses on Pinky's back with his knee. Yells at the top of his voice.*) Eat the dirt! Eat!

The other two boys hold Pinky tight by his arms. His face is pressed against the soft ground. He is gratified it is soft. The boy in the middle rubs his head on the ground back and forth. Some dirt gets inside Pinky's mouth. He tastes it and involuntarily swallows it. He is surprised it doesn't taste bad. It is bland like the oatmeal porridge he is obliged to eat every morning.

The boy in the middle (*rubbing Pinky's face in the dirt, yelling*): Eat! Eat! (*After a pause.*) Are you eating it?

Pinky (*mumbling back*): Yes.

The boy in the middle: Is it good?

Pinky (*mumbling back again*): Yes. (*His words are muffled by the dirt in his mouth.*)

The boy in the middle grows wild. He jumps up and presses harder on Pinky's back with his knee. He turns Pinky's head so that his face is free.

The boy in the middle (*growing wild, at the top of his voice*): You will eat worms now! (*After a few seconds' pause.*) Will you?

Pinky (*thinking earth worms must taste like earth and therefore wouldn't taste bad, meekly*): Yes.

The boy in the middle looks around on the ground to search for an earthworm. He doesn't see one and keeps on looking. The boy on his right does the same. He doesn't see any so he lets go of Pinky's arm and gets up too look for one. The boy in the middle presses down harder on Pinky's back with his knee. They all wait for the boy who went away to come.

4. numbers

A long and narrow windowless room. The walls and ceiling painted a shiny off-white. A light gray vinyl tile floor with black streaks in it to simulate and therefore mask dirt. A light gray metal door with a stainless steel handle in the corner of one of the longer walls. Two rows of neon lights behind plastic covers running down the middle of the ceiling almost the whole length of the room. The room therefore very bright.

A long off-white Formica-topped table with tubular stainless steel legs in the middle of the room its longer side parallel to the longer walls. It looks inappropriate because its length is much shorter than that of the walls. It is almost as if the table stood at a slight angle to the walls and begs to be straightened out. Two matching chairs (matching each other as well as the table) at the table facing each other across the narrower side.

The director in the chair facing the door holding a calculator in his hand, Pinky on the other side next to the chair facing the director while standing up, a ballpoint pen in his hand, a writing pad on the table in front of him.

The director a tall thin man with black hair slicked down over his skull and parted in the middle, a bony face, black crossed eyes, and a gap between his two top front teeth as if a model for the part in his hair to match. Speaks in a mushy nasal voice and lisps. Dressed in a black tight-fitting three-pieced suit, a white shirt, and a black tie. Looks like an undertaker.

The director: OK Pinky now multiply 12345 by 6789. *(After a pause, when Pinky bends down ready to write the answer down on the pad.)* Write the two numberth down firtht and then the anthwer.

Pinky does as he is told, without any sign of hesitation between the second and third numbers, putting down 83810205 as the answer. He then straightens up.

The director in the meantime enters the two numbers on the calculator, obtains the product, cranes his neck over to look at the pad, turns the latter a little so as to better see it, scrutinizes with his crossed eyes the page, has trouble reading from it (because of the position or because of being cross-eyed?), finally is able to read the number Pinky wrote down as the product, compares it with the one he obtained, and sees they are the same.

The director (*with some reluctance*): You're right. (*Thinks for a while. Continues.*) OK now multiply 6789 by (*A longish pause.*) 99999.

Pinky writes the two numbers down and then immediately the product 678893211. After doing it he turns the pad about forty-five degrees for the director to be able to better read from it, and straightens up.

The director races to enter the two numbers on the calculator, obtains 678793212 as the answer, checks it with that of Pinky's, has less trouble reading it this time, sees they are different, is about to say something but decides to reenter the numbers on the calculator again in case he made a mistake (He did—he entered 6788 for the first number.), reenters the numbers correctly, obtains the product, compares it with that of Pinky's, and sees they are the same. He is visibly amazed.

The director (*full of respect*): How do you do it Pinky? Do you like thee what the numberth should be on paper if you were multiplying them and then add them up in your head?

Pinky (*calmly*):   No, it's like the numbers you give me are two
planes that fit together on one side and I have to get a third one
to fill the gap between them... to complete the shape... make it
one plane.... It's easy. I don't even have to think about it.... I just
know what's to go into the slot... Sometimes I have to juggle it
around a little but usually I get it right away.... I don't know how
it happens. But it's easy.

The director: You did it with addition and thubtraction and now
multiplication. Can you do it also with division.

Pinky (*nonchalantly*): Yes.

The director (*leaning back, his crossed eyes wide open; they look even
more crossed than before*): It'th amathing. (*After a pause.*) You
should be a mathematician. (*After a pause.*) Ith that what you
want to be?

Pinky (*firmly*): No.

The director (*amazed*): You don't want to be a mathematician?...
With you ability with numberth?... Why not?

Pinky: I find it boring. Numbers are boring. I don't like math.

The director *(curious)*: What do you want to be then?

Pinky *(quickly and firmly)*: A tinker.

The director *(not understanding)*: A thinker?

Pinky *(annoyed)*: No, a TINKER...maker of tin cans... pots.... Like they used to make them in the old days.

The director *(amazed)*: Maker of potth?... *(Still more amazed.)* But why?

Pinky *(with utmost assuredness)*: Because it makes a wonderful sound.... Hitting tin sheet with a hammer.... And then taking these flat forms and turning them into round ones.... Joining them together.... It's like with the numbers except it's better.... You can touch them.... I'd do it all day long.... Sitting on my stool and hammering away... and cutting and bending.... With no one bothering me.... Just me and the hammer and the sheet metal and shears.

The director *(still more amazed)*: Do you do it now in your thpare time... in thecret... with no-ne watching?

Pinky: No. I've done it a little a few times.... Like hitting tin cans with a stick or a stone... and bending a flat piece.... But I imagine it.... It's like doing it for real. It's fun too.

5. an angel

Pinky's dream.

It is a bright if frosty winter day. The sun is blazing and there is fresh snow all around.

He is lying on his back in the snow spreading his legs wide and closing them while moving his arms up and down and thrashing with them in the snow over and over again making an angel. He is keeping his eyes closed because the sun is blinding him.

Suddenly he feels a shadow on his face. He will be able to open his eyes without being blinded by the sun. He opens them and looks.

There is a tall human figure standing over him shielding him from the sun. It is dressed in a long white robe, has something white and rounded sticking up from behind its shoulders, and a circle is hovering over it on top. It is an angel with a halo over his head!

He is overjoyed. He has been waiting for one to come to his rescue and his wish has finally come true.

He tries to sit up and the angel reaches down with his hand and helps him get up. The angel's hand is big, strong, and warm, exactly what he would like it to be.

As he stands up and looks closer he realizes the angel is actually a man dressed up as one. The robe is a long white garment resembling a night shirt, the wings are made from shredded white paper tissue glued onto solid forms, and the halo is a metal hoop painted gold with a rod supporting it in the back. Big wing-tipped shoes stick out on the bottom from under the shirt the man is wearing and you can see the cuffs of thick tweed cloth pants above them. The man has short curly golden hair, golden eyebrows, and a pleasant fleshy face. Something like gold dust sparkles on his cheeks—a faint stubble. He hasn't shaved for a few days. His mouth is spread wide in a friendly smile and his eyes twinkle with kindness. They too seem golden.

He is overjoyed. He is not in the least disappointed the angel is a man. On he contrary he feels it might be better it is so. It is more real. He waits for what the man will do.

The man had let go of his hand as he stood up and now he takes it again and says something he doesn't quite understand. It may have been said in a foreign language. But still he has a feeling the man said he would take him somewhere. He merely can't repeat the words.

The man must have said that because he does lead him away.

They walk down the street, the man holding him by the hand. He feels the strength and warmth of the man's hand and is full of joy. He has never been so happy before. He can't think of anything else he might want.

The snow is blinding white in the bright sun and he can barely make out his surroundings. They are like the world in an overexposed photograph. Still he is aware they are walking down a residential street. There are single-storied houses behind picket fences on both sides and they pass them one by one.

They come up to one house and the man stops, opens the gate in the fence, and lets him pass through it before he does so himself. The house is essentially like all the others they have passed—single-storied, made from white clapboards, with a door in the center and windows on both sides of it. The door is partly open.

They walk down the path leading to the door, the man pushes the latter open, and lets him go first. Then he follows him and closes the door.

There must be a party going on inside because the place is full of people. They throng in the hallway and the rest of the house seems to be just as full. Cigarette smoke fills the air and the sound of human voices mingles with it as if another kind of smoke. It is very warm.

The man says something to him and he again cannot make out the words, this time probably because of the noise. The man notices this and shows with gestures what he meant—he is going to take off his costume. He thinks this is because it is so warm in the house. He would be uncomfortable dressed as he is.

He nods indicating that he understands what he man has said implying that he has nothing against it.

The man goes off into the crowd and he remains standing by the door.

Time passes and he remains standing in the same spot. He starts worrying—should he go looking for the man? Did the man want him to follow him and he merely didn't realize it?

He feels this must be the case and goes off into the crowd as the man had done.

The place is huge, more like a public building than a private home. There are many rooms and they are all filled with people. The latter stand in groups talking to each other and gesticulating. They are all adult men and they pay no attention to him. It is as if he didn't exist.

He grows desperate by the minute. Where is the man? He came to rescue him and now he is gone. What could have happened to him?

Suddenly he notices the man. He stands in a group of some five or six men talking to each other. He clearly knows them and they must have corralled him as he was walking by and he hasn't been able to get away to come back to him.

He stops a few feet away from the group and waits for the man to notice him. As soon as this happens the man will join him.

He stands directly opposite the man facing him. There are a couple of men between them with their backs to him but the man will have no problem seeing him as soon as he turns his face forward. At the moment he is looking to his right talking to someone. Suddenly he turns his head straight and looks in his eyes.

From the expression in them he knows the man has recognized him. He remembers the man's kind look and smile and is sure they will reappear any second.

This doesn't happen however. The man quickly turns his face to the right and resumes talking as before. He pretends not to have seen him. He will not come back to him.

A vast abyss opens up inside him. He is all alone among these strangers. What is he going to do?

6. brian o'brien

The phone rings, the bartender goes over to where it hangs on the wall in the corner next to the bar, picks up the receiver, presses to his ear, listens for a few seconds, says, Yeah, hold on a second, takes the receiver away from his ear, and calls out to Pinky's father, It's for you O'Brien.

Pinky's father stirs on the high bar stool on which he sits as if turning over in bed and asks in a muffled slurred voice as if his mouth were stuffed with a thick wool sock, Who is it?

Some guy with a German accent, the man answers.

A German accent? Pinky's father screws up his face and with disgust on it gets off the stool nearly falling down in the process and walks in an unsteady gait in an uneven line, equivalent to a dotted line on paper, to the phone which looks like an ear tightly pressed to the wall trying to hear what is happening on the other side of it. He was the only one at the bar and it is hard to tell if it is people sitting in the darkness at the few tables under the wall on the left or shadows that have merged with the furniture.

The receiver hangs limp along the wall on its wire like a paralyzed arm. The bartender has gone over to his customary spot at that end of the bar and stands with arms folded on his chest following Pinky's father with his eyes.

Pinky's father reaches the phone, takes a hold of the receiver, presses it to his ear, and in the same slurred voice says, Hallo.

The following monologue ensues punctuated by periods of silence. You cannot hear what the voice on the other end is saying.

It's Brian, yeah.

Brief silence.

Oh it's bloody you!

Longer silence.

Why the foock do you have to resort to these foockin subterfuges to make me coom to the phone. I'd have coom anyway.

Shorter silence.

I don't have the foockin mooney!... I told you I'd pi you bahck when I got it. But right now I haven't got it. I don't have it! Don't you oonderstand?

Brief silence.

Soon.

Brief silence.

Very, very soon.

I'm workin on it. The prospects are good. I'll have it soon.

Longer silence.

I can't give you the foockin dough if I haven't got it. Right?... You'll be the first I pi off when I get it. I promise. Word of honor. You can count on me.

Brief silence.

Don't give me that shit. When I tell you, you can count on me you can count on me. You know that.

Brief silence.

You're a blooddy schmoock yourself, you foockin schmoock! Bothering me at all hours of di and night as if I didn't know I owes you money. I'm not denyin it. I'm an honorable person. I'll pi you bahck as soon as I have it. And I'm working on getting it and will have it soon. I told you that. So leave me alone you blooddy schmoock!

He slams the receiver down with a bang on the hook, miraculously it stays there, he turns away from the wall, and heads back to his stool which is patiently waiting for him next to the bar where he has left it. It is surprising it hasn't wandered off somewhere.

His return trip resembles very closely the one in the opposite direction in its plan but only approximately it its execution.

Still he makes it to the stool, climbs up on it as if onto a steep hill, makes himself comfortable (safe) on it, pushes forward the empty glass that is standing on the bar in front of him, and says to the bartender, Give me another one Johnny.

No O'Brien, the man replies shaking his head, You've had too many already.

One more please Johnny, Pinky's father pleads, his voice still muffled but in a different way, more delicately, as if by a silk handkerchief.

No Brian, no, the bartender says calmly barely stirring in his spot. You've had enough for tonight. Go home and sleep it off.

Pinky's father is suddenly energized as if having gotten sober. His face swells up and turns red.

Just another foockin shot John! He shouts, white spittle like popcorn flying out of his mouth. He picks up the empty glass and slams it down hard on the counter.

The glass makes a hard loud sound which suddenly changes into a different, pathetically weak one. The glass breaks and looks like a bunch of smashed ice cubes on top of the counter.

Pinky's father brings his hand close to his eyes and looks at it with curiosity as if at an object he has just found. He seems to have never seen it. His palm is wet and oozes blood in a few places.

See what you've done to me you foockin schmoock, he says accusingly looking at the bartender and stretching his hand out to him. You made me cut my blooddy hand!

The bartender calmly walks out from behind the bar, comes up to Pinky's father, grabs him with his left hand by the collar of his jacket, and pulls him off the stool.

You're a schmuck O'Brien, he says as he easily turns him around in the direction of the door. You're going home.

Pinky's father tries to free himself from the bartender's grip emitting protesting sounds but the man is too strong for him. He towers by nearly a full head over him.

The bartender grabs Pinky's father with his right hand by the seat of his pants, pushes him to the outside door, opens the latter with his foot, and shoves Pinky's father out into the street without a word. The door closes by itself.

Pinky's father sprawls face down on the sidewalk.

He lies still for a few seconds, raises himself up on his arms, and looks around. He has forgotten about cutting his hand and feels no pain in it.

The street is empty in both directions as far as he can see except for the cars parked close to each other along the curb on both sides.

Suddenly he sees in the middle of the block to his left a strange sight—a car is cutting across it perpendicularly as if it were driving down a road. What will happen when it comes to the car parked on the other side? Will it try driving through it? He wonders.

He blinks hard and opens his eyes as wide as he can to make sure he is seeing right. The sight doesn't change.

7. marle

Suddenly a whole big compound emerged on his left he had never seen before—a house, a huge barn-like structure, and a yard, all behind a tall picket fence. He was sure he had walked through this neighborhood before but inexplicably had not noticed the place. It seemed to have been deposited there like a prop on a stage. Could it really have been built in the little time that had elapsed since he had passed through the neighborhood the last time? It was impossible. It didn't look brand new. In fact it looked old.

Pinky decided not to worry about what all this meant, walked on a few more steps until he passed the gate, stopped, turned left, and looked. The fence was short enough for him to be able to see over it.

The house stood with its side toward the street and its front to the yard. It was single-storied, had siding made of treated dark brown wood, a tall shingled roof, and a porch that ran its whole length from one side to the other. The roof over the porch was supported by thin posts. The barn—barn-like structure—was twice as tall as the house, had a similar shingled roof, and was built out of the same kind of treated dark brown wooden boards as the siding on the house. It had a huge sliding door which was open showing its dark cavernous inside. Faint outlines of objects such as wheelbarrows, carts, paper sacks filled with something, spades, hoes, rakes, etc. could be seen emerging out of the darkness close to the door like creatures waking reluctantly from deep sleep. The darkness deep inside was close in color to that of the barn as if trying hard to match it. The picket fence was stained the same color as the siding of the house and the barn.

It had rained during the night and the ground in the yard was dark, likewise close in color to that of the house, the barn, and the fence as if also trying hard to match it. It looked fertile and seemed to crave to sprout vegetation of any kind.

Plants of various kinds in pots big and small stood neatly arranged on the ground starting from about the middle of the yard to the right and extending along the side of the barn all the way to the back.

A tall trim male figure emerged out of the darkness inside the barn almost the instant Pinky stopped and walked toward the plants on the right. The man had thick but well-trimmed gray hair, a pleasant attractive face, and looked in his mid fifties. He wore a dark blue jumpsuit and on his feet tall black rubber boots.

He walked in among the plants, picked up the end of a black garden hose that lay on the ground, and started watering the plants around him. Pinky hadn't noticed it until then. There was a nozzle on the end of the hose and the man merely opened it.

The water flowed in a gentle curving stream over the plants and they looked like placid animals eagerly drinking it up. They seemed to have been waiting for the man to come to water them.

There was something calming in what was happening and Pinky felt himself growing all soft inside. Eventually unable to stop the emotions that were surging up in him and accepting the phrase that popped up in his mind he asked the man, Are you a gardener?

The man instantly turned around and said smiling, Vat else do you seenk I could be? He had been clearly aware of Pinky's presence and seemed to have waited for him to speak. He spoke with a German accent.

I just said it to say something, Pinky replied smiling himself, aware there was no derision in the man's words. They look so happy.... I mean the plants drinking the water. They have been waiting for it.

Dey haf been, the man replied still smiling and continuing to water the plants. Like all creatures dey need eet.

Vood you like to haf some vahter? He asked suddenly changing the subject.

Pinky stayed silent for an instant as if in a state of shock but then pulled himself together and replied with joy in his voice, Yes, I would. I am thirsty in fact. Thank you.

Marie, the man yelled in the direction of the house, for an instant directing the water onto the ground, Breeng heem some vahter.

Seconds after the man had spoken a slender female figure stepped out of the house. (Its door had been open all along. Pinky merely hadnt noticed it.) It was a girl about fourteen years old with blond almost white hair tied into braids and dressed in a white embroidered short-sleeved blouse, a short blue skirt, and a red apron over it. She had sandals on her bare feet.

What did you say? She called out. Her voice betrayed no accent.

Breeng de yoong man a glass of aloe vahter, the man repeated having turned his face to the girl, now watering a plant again.

Right away, the girl replied cheerfully and ran back into the house.

Aloe vera juice ees good for you, the man explained. I grow aloe vera plants and vee put fresh juice een de vahter. Eet ees good for de body... and de soul. He concluded.

Yes, Pinky said closing his eyes unable to continue. He was afraid he was going to fall asleep.

When he opened his eyes the girl stood in front of him extending a tall glass filled with clear liquid over the fence.

He took it and bowing his head as if before something holy pressed his lips to it and drank. The liquid streamed like the awareness of some important good news to him.

She ees my daughter, he heard the man say. Her real name ees Grete but I call her Marie. It goes better vit her looks.

Pinky stopped drinking and moved the glass slightly away from his lips. He planned to continue drinking again. He saw the world through the space as if through a crack in the door.

The man had turned off the water and stood with the hose in his hand looking in his direction.

She ees young now but one day she veell grow up and marry a nice yoong gentleman like you, he said smiling.

With the corner of his eye Pinky saw the girl's face across the fence—her neatly combed flaxen hair, her bulging porcelain forehead, her blue cornflower eyes under the curving eyebrows a little darker than the hair as if temporarily in a shade, her snow-white teeth gleaming iridescent between the pink lips parted in a smile.

For an instant he felt himself turn red with embarrassment but then that stopped and the reverse took place. He grew colder and colder turning white with fear. A vast chasm was opening inside him into which he was going to fall. He was afraid he would faint.

8. first date

A square, nearly cubical room with the vertical dimension slightly smaller than the horizontal ones. The walls and ceiling painted a shiny light gray. A slightly lighter vinyl tile floor with black streaks in it to simulate and therefore mask dirt. A metal door of a darker gray than the walls and with a stainless steel knob leading into the corridor in the middle of one of the walls. A similar narrower door leading to a closet in the corner on the left. Two tall curtainless windows in the wall opposite the one with the first door with a gloomy late early fall afternoon outside them, the light streaming in through them blending in with the color of the walls. A stainless steel hospital bed between the windows, its headboard against the wall. A matching stainless steel bed stand on its left. A few small ill-defined objects like shadows of real objects on top of it. A stainless steel container looking like a bedpan underneath. A stainless steel chair matching the bed next to the window on the left facing the bed.

A woman (young/middle-aged?) is sitting in the chair, her head bent down watching herself knit. She has an unnaturally small as if shrunken head with greasy looking dark hair tightly stretched over it like a sleazy fabric about to come apart and tied into a tight knot-like chignon in the back, a long thin neck, bulging black eyes, a hollow face with a long nose, and a small receding chin.

She is dressed in a loose faded flowery gray-blue-pink dress with what seems like nothing underneath. Her chest is caved in with the dress lose over it like a slack sail on a boat and betrays no sign of breasts. Her body is extremely thin with bones seeming to have been shoved in disarray under the dress like stolen items (silverware) hastily into a sack.

The object she is knitting is a long and narrow strip of pink wool which covers her lap and curls up over her feet on the floor like a cat. A ball of pink yarn lies on her lap partly hidden by the object she is knitting. The needles seem aluminum and they flash coldly in the light coming in through the window making painful ear-jarring sounds like the breaking of bones.

Pinky is standing in front of the woman partly turned left.

Pinky (*after a long silence*): What's your name?

The woman (*calmly, without raising her head, here and throughout the conversation unless otherwise indicated*): Alma.

Pinky (*slightly excited*): Alba? Like the duchess of Alba Goya painted?

The woman: No, Alma, meaning soul in Latin.

Pinky (*more excited*): Oh that's wonderful.... Were your parents like very religious... spiritual... that they named you Soul?

The woman: No. I mean they were somewhat spiritual... religious... but this had nothing to do with my name. They named me after Alma Mahler, the wife of Gustav Mahler. My parents came from Germany. My family name is Schindler which was Alma Mahler's maiden name and my mother was a musicologist who specialized in Mahler. So that was why they chose the name for me. (*After a brief pause.*) But we weren't related to those Schindlers. They were Austrians. It's just a coincidence. (*After a longish pause.*) My middle name is Manon which was the name of Alma Mahler's daughter by the famous architect Walter Gropius whom Alma married after her first husband died. My father was an architect and a great admirer of Gropius so he chose that name for me. (*After a brief pause.*) Their daughter... Manon... died of polio at the age of eighteen. (*After a slightly longer pause.*) I too had polio when I was a teenager. (*After a very brief pause.*) But it had nothing to do with my being called Manon. Many kids got polio in those days... before they got the vaccine.

Pinky has wondered about the woman's physical condition from the moment he saw her and now thinks he has the answer.

Pinky (*sure he is right, glad to have solved the mystery*): Are you like paralyzed from having had polio?... You can't walk?

The woman (*calmly*): No. I'm alright. I can walk with no problems. There were some aftereffects at first but I got over them. I was lucky. (*Changing the subject and lifting her eyes from her knitting for an instant.*) And what is your name?

Pinky (*disappointed by her answer but his mind immediately occupied by the new topic which is dear to him, quickly*): Pinky. (*Remembers the connection between his and the woman's surnames. Enthusiastically.*) My last name is also German—Schmuck. (*Adds very quickly.*) It means jewel in German. My father was... is... German. He is a nobleman and lives in Germany... in a castle on the Rhine.

The woman (*quietly*): Yes I know that Schmuck means a jewel in German... or a decoration...like a Christmas decoration.... My parents taught me that. It's pronounced shmook.

Pinky (*very gratified*): Yes. That's right.

The woman: And why did they call you Pinky?

Pinky *(quickly)*: Oh, my mother chose it. *(Almost without a pause.)* I don't know why she did it. Maybe because I was small... and pink. *(Quickly.)* No, it couldn't have been that. I was a blue baby.... I'll have to ask her when she gets back. She's away on a long trip.

The answer satisfies the woman. She asks no further questions and goes on knitting. Silence reigns in the room once again punctuated by the regular clanking of the needles.

Pinky notices for the first time there is no sign of crutches or canes anywhere in the room which should have made it clear to him the woman isn't paralyzed. He blames himself for his inattention. He thinks he is stupid. Then he remembers there is another thing he doesn't know—what is the woman knitting? He has been wondering about it also from the beginning.

Pinky *(deciding to find out, curious)*:   What are you knitting? *(Unexpectedly finds a possible answer to his question. Decides to convey this information to the woman.)*   Baby's clothes? (*Then another possibility unexpectedly surfaces in his mind and he decides to pursue it. Its nature doesn't in the least bother him.)*)   Are you pregnant?

The woman *(quietly)*: No. I'm not knitting baby's clothes. They don't look like that. *(Smiling barely perceptibly but still not lifting her eyes from her work, with irony.)* I'm not pregnant. I can't have babies. I'm too weak for it... probably because I had polio. *(Goes back to the first question.)* I knit because I suffer from Turret's syndrome. If I don't knit I twitch. Knitting stops it for me. *(After a pause.)* See?

She stops knitting, lifts her head, and turns her face to Pinky.

Instantly it is distorted by a powerful twitch. Her mouth opens wide. Her lips retract. Her teeth stick out. Her lower jaw moves way over to the left. Her right eye opens real wide. It bulges. Her left eye nearly closes. The skin around it creases. It looks like she is trying to wink at Pinky while planning to bite him at the same time. She is like a portrait of a nasty woman by Picasso that has come alive.

Pinky shudders and wants to jump back so as not to be bitten but catches himself in time. He understands what is happening. He is not put off by the woman's behavior. On the contrary he feels closer to her.

The woman *(bending her head down and resuming her knitting; there is no sign of the twitch left on her face)*: I knit a long piece like this and then unravel it and knit again. I still have a way to go.

She lifts the ball of yarn from her lap and quickly shows it to
Pinky without raising her head. It is still sizeable. She puts the
ball back in its place and goes back to knitting instantly.

Pinky (not paying much attention to what she is saying and doing,
anxious to get out what is on his mind): It's very interesting that you
don't twitch when you knit. I have a similar situation. I stutter
when I don't stand up. That's why I try to stand up as much as I
can when I'm speaking.... Look. (He squats down.) See what
happens? (After a brief pause.) I am trying to speak right now.
(Stops. There is puzzlement on his face. After a longish pause.) It's
strange.... I'm not sttttuttering rrrright now.... I mean I
wassssn't.... Now I am ssssomewhat.... (After a pause, when he
stands up.) It must have been the strain of squatting down... the
way I sat. It must have been the same as if I were standing up.
(After a pause.) See.... Now it's ggggone. (After a pause.) Almost
gone.... (With relief, smiling.) Now it's gone completely.

The woman (calmly; she has been watching him from under her
eyebrows without interrupting her knitting): Yes, strain must have
something to do with it. But psychological involvement too.
(After a pause.) Anyway for me knitting works perfectly.

Pinky (in full empathy with the woman, forgetting about his failed
experiment): You're lucky that you can control it like that by

yourself. As I understand it most people have to take drugs and they don't work much of the time.

The woman: Yes. Most of the time nothing works. (*After a pause.*) I'm lucky.

She continues her knitting in silence.

Pinky watches the needles flash periodically and hears their painful clanking. He searches his mind for other topics he might want to explore with the woman but finds none. He has found out everything he might have wanted to know about her and discussed all topics of interest to him. He decides to leave.

Pinky: I guess I will leave now.

The woman (*calmly*): Yes. Alright. (*After a pause.*) You know your way out.

Pinky: Yes. (*After a pause.*) Right at the door, down the corridor, down the stairs, turn right, and out the front door.

The woman: That's right.

Pinky: And I turn right when I'm outside.

The woman: That's right.... Turn right. You came from that direction. I watched you coming in.

9. numbers again

Schmuck! His name cracked loud like a bullwhip snapping behind him its end reaching him almost across the whole length of the corridor leaving a painful sting on his consciousness.

He turned around abruptly and looked.

What the hell is this mess in Mrs. Schreck's room? The man bellowed spreading his arms wide for an instant before returning them to his sides. They seemed the equivalent of exclamation points on a page. He was from one of the English-speaking Caribbean countries and spoke with the sing-song accent typical of those regions.

The tall and slender figure of his supervisor stood out sharp black against the blinding white background—they were doing some extensive electrical work in the building and the lights had been turned off in the corridors all morning—badly eroded along the edges however like a steep river bank by a swift-flowing current so that it seemed it might crumble eventually and perhaps even any minute. Up front its horizontal version was a still longer and thinner but merely an ill-defined stain on the shiny mirror-like floor. He was sure he looked the same way in the man's eyes except a lot shorter and wider in both directions—vertically and horizontally. The outside wall on this side of the building was solid glass the same as on the other one.

Although ostensibly a question the sentence clearly didn't require an answer but a different response and Pinky started off in his supervisor's direction his head bowed, laboriously trudging along the hard floor as if walking through deep mud.

The room was on the left where the man stood and they both squeezed almost at the same time through the wide door into it, Pinky a fraction of a step ahead. It was square and small with a low ceiling and no windows, illuminated by a bank of neon lights, its walls painted dark green. The door to the bathroom was in the near corner on the left and the bed stood with its headboard against that wall in the center. A bed stand huddled against it and the wall on its near side. On the other side of the bed in the far corner on the left was another door—that to the closet.

A row of stainless steel bedpans, perhaps a dozen of them, stood neatly lined up under the bed which was piled some three feet high with likewise neatly folded sheets with crisp edges as if they had been freshly ironed, arranged in four stacks. They weren't fresh because stains were visible on some of them—red, brown, yellow, etc, in other words soiled with blood, feces, urine, and different kinds of food.

Why in God's name have you put all these things in this room mahn? The man asked in an exasperated voice. This isn't a storage room. It belongs to a patient. You should have taken the things downstairs.

And why have you folded the sheets up so neatly? He went on. They have to be washed and if you put them folded like that in the machine they won't wash properly. You'll have to unfold them all over again. It'll take time. He continued after a pause, And how much time it must have taken you to fold them neatly like that?! You can't waste your time on such matters. You have zillions of other things to do.

The elevator hasn't worked all morning and I didn't want to run down with just a couple of these things at a time, Pinky explained calmly. So I thought I'd put them all here together and take a whole bunch of them at once.

But why did you fold the sheets? The man asked pleadingly. It's a total waste of time. And you'll have to unfold them again.

When I put them in even planes like that, Pinky said, I can keep better track of them. Just by looking at them for instance I know right away how many of them are there—one hundred twenty-three. Plus the eleven bedpans on the floor I have one hundred thirty-four items to take down. It's easier for me to do my job that way. I know where I stand.

My God, you and your numbers, the man said. I don't see why you have to keep track of everything. But why are you using Mrs. Schreck's room? He went on.

By the way where is she? He suddenly changed the subject.

They took her away, Pinky replied calmly.

Took her away? The man asked surprised. Who did? Where?

Some men with masks. I don't know where, Pinky went on as before.

Men with masks?! The man exclaimed alarmed. You mean she was kidnapped?

I don't know if she was kidnapped, Pinky said. She didn't seem to protest.

Did they take her to the operating room?   The man asked concerned. Were they in green?

No, they were not in green. They were in black and had black masks on their faces, Pinky replied.

So she was kidnapped! The man exclaimed.

I don't think so, Pinky said calmly. As I said she didn't protest. Maybe they were undertakers.... Came to bury her.... Maybe she was dead.... She didn't move at all when they wheeled her away. And they were all in black.

Did they take her in the wheelchair? The man asked in a calmer voice.

Yes, Pinky said concisely.

And you said they were all in black? The man continued.

Yes, Pinky said again.

Are you sure they didn't have white masks on their faces like those you wear to protect yourself or others from infection? The man went on.

Pinky pondered a little and finally said, They might have.... Some of them at least did.... Probably. (After a long pause.) For sure.

Were they all men? The man asked hopefully.

Yes, Pinky replied vigorously without any hesitation. And big and strong too... husky.

Did they have black beards? The man asked with even greater hope.

They could have, Pinky answered. Some of them did for sure, he added after further thinking. Those without masks.

And those with masks... white masks... had black beards sticking out from under them? The man said quickly as if afraid something important would get away from him if he didn't hurry, his voice like the sky gradually clearing up. And there were five of them? He concluded, his voice fully clear.

Yes, Pinky said after a few seconds' hesitation. And that made it look like they wore black masks. And those that didn't have white masks looked like they wore black masks because they had thick black beards.... And yes, there were five of them, he said at the end in a firm satisfied voice.

Oh, don't you see what happened? The man laughed, his face dissolving in a smile. You're a real case Pinky. You gave me some scare.... Those were Mrs. Schreck's sons mahn. They came and took her to the cafeteria. You know the family's Orthodox Jewish and they wear black clothes and the men all wear beards.

This happened when? The man asked after a pause. A while ago?

A while ago, Pinky agreed.

We'd better get going, Pinky mahn, the man said in an alarmed voice. They can be back any minute. We'd better move these things out. You know what a terror Mrs. Schreck is. She will raise hell if she sees all these things in her room... the dirty sheets on the bed and the bedpans....

I'll give you a hand, he said quickly stepping up to the bed and picking out a manageable stack of sheets from the rightmost of the four big ones. We'll put them in the corridor near the elevator so that you can take them down when it's working.

Pinky hadn't noticed Mrs. Schreck was a terror in spite of her name. She had been kind to him perhaps because of the similarity of their names.   Nonetheless he agreed to go along with his supervisor's plan and stepped up to the leftmost stack. It was better to be safe. Without hesitation he stuck his left hand between the fifteenth and sixteenth sheet from the bottom while putting his right one on top to hold them in place. This stack the same as the next two had thirty-one sheets in it so he would have one less to take the next time.

10. second date

Once again a square, nearly cubical room, with the vertical dimension slightly smaller than the horizontal ones. The walls and ceiling painted a shiny off white. A light gray vinyl tile floor. A metal door of a darker gray than the floor with a stainless steel knob leading into the corridor in the middle of one of the walls. An identical door leading to a closet in the corner on the left. Two tall curtainless windows in the wall opposite to the one with the first door with a gloomy early late fall morning outside them, the light streaming in through them blending in with the color of the walls. A stainless steel exceptionally tall hospital bed, its extendable legs lengthened about a foot, piled still higher with bedclothes and covered with a shiny silvery bedspread between the windows, its headboard against the wall. Just looking at it makes one feel uneasy as if standing on top of a tall mountain peak with precipices all around. A matching stainless steel bed stand on its left its legs extended about as much as those of the bed. A few small ill-defined objects like shadows of real objects on top of it. Two steel containers one looking like a bedpan and the other one like a mixing bowl underneath. A spoon is sticking out over the edge of the latter.

A young woman (girl?) is sitting on top of the bed in its middle with her legs crossed, her back turned to the wall with the closet door. She is very small and skinny with thin straight flaxen hair braided into two ratty pigtails tied together with rubber bands at the end, lively blue eyes, a light complexion, a freckled face, and a thin wide mouth. Something whitish is gathered around the corners of her mouth and on her chin similar to but too light for freckles. She is wearing a loose long short-sleeved white garment (a nightshirt/dress?) with tiny blue flowers on it. Where her breasts should be the nightshirt/dress sticks up barely noticeably crinkled like the little paper umbrellas used to decorate tropical cocktail drinks.

Pinky is standing by the side of the bed in front of the woman/girl partly turned left.

Pinky (*after a long silence*): What's your name?

The woman/girl (*cheerfully*): Winky.

Pinky (*surprised*): Winnie?

The woman/girl (*emphatic but unperturbed*): No. Winky.

Pinky (*excited*): Winky?... That's wonderful. (*After a pause.*) Is it a nickname?... I mean like is your real name Wink?

The woman/girl (*laughing*): No, it's for Periwinkle. That's my real name. (*After a pause.*) Like my eyes (*Points to them.*) and these flowers. (*Points to the nightshirt/dress, giggles.*) Periwinky-Winky. (*Almost without a pause.*) And yours?... I mean what's your name?

Pinky: Pinky.

The woman/girl (*slapping her hands together, laughing*): Oh, that's wonderful! It goes so well with mine!... (*Giggles.*) Pinky-Winky, Winky-Pinky. (*Continues giggling.*)

Pinky (*surprised*): Yes... Pinky-Winky. (*After a pause, smiling.*) It's nice.... I'm surprised I didn't notice it myself.

Silence follows with the girl fidgeting on top of the bed breathing heavily through her nose and chewing on the end of one of her braids.

Pinky (*after a long deliberation*): What did you have for breakfast?

The woman/girl (*cheerfully again, giggling*): Oatmeal porridge with milk. (*Without a pause.*) And you?

Pinky (*cheerful himself this time*): Oatmeal porridge with milk too. It's amazing. We're so similar. (*After a brief pause.*) I love it. I have it every morning. And you?

The woman/girl (*cheerfully, giggling*): I do too.... I mean I love it and I have it every morning. (*After a brief pause, pointing downward.*) There's this morning's bowl under the bed. They still haven't taken it away.

Pinky quickly glances under the bed without bending down, sees the bowl next to the bedpan, then looks at the woman's/girl's face, notices the light flecks around her mouth, and realizes what they are.

Pinky: You still have some of it on your face... around your mouth and on your chin. (*Points to them.*)

The woman/girl (*licking and rubbing her face around her mouth clean, laughing*): Oooo! I'm a bad girl. (*Laughs some more.*) I haven't washed up yet.

Pinky doesn't know what to say. He has satisfied all of his curiosity. Silence reigns again in the room with the girl fidgeting around on top of the bed and breathing heavily through her nose sounding surprisingly loud for someone her size. This time she has left her braid alone.

Pinky (*glad to have managed to come up with something*): Do you have a brother?

The woman/girl: No. I don't.

Pinky (*without a pause*): Do you think your brother would have liked oatmeal porridge with milk if you had one?

The woman/girl (*quickly*): Yes, I'm sure he would have. Both of my parents like it and so do I so he would have liked it too. I'm sure of that. It must be genetic. (*After a pause.*) And you, do you have a brother?

Pinky: No. I don't.

The woman/girl: Do you think though your brother would have liked oatmeal porridge with milk if you had one?

Pinky (*serious*): I'm not sure but he probably would have. I know that my father loves oatmeal porridge with milk. He lives in Germany in a castle on the Rhine and they eat a lot of oatmeal porridge there... because it's healthy. Germans are very health conscious and they are careful with their diet. And I love it too. (*After a pause.*) My mother doesn't eat it all the time but sometimes she does. She probably likes it but she travels a lot and doesn't have a chance to eat it more often. (*After a longer pause.*) I'll ask her if she likes it when she comes back. She's away on a long trip. (*After a pause.*) But I'm pretty sure my brother would have liked oatmeal porridge with milk if I had one. If I got the taste for it from either my father or both of my parents then it's almost certain he would have too.

A realization about what the woman's/girl's name implies suddenly pushes its way into his mind. He drops what he has been talking about and eagerly pursues the new subject.

Pinky (*with great curiosity*): But do you like to wink a lot because of your name?.... I mean did they also call you Winky because you like to wink?

The woman/girl (*laughing heartily*): Yes I do like to wink a lot. I do it all the time. See.... (*She winks very pronouncedly at Pinky. Suddenly apparently as an afterthought she winks once again and stretches her arms out to him.*) Come on climb up on the bed.

Pinky is taken aback by the proposition, momentarily not understanding what it means. Then he realizes what it entails and feels chills run up his spine. The prospect terrifies him.

Pinky (*nervous, shuddering*): It's too high. I can't. I'm afraid of heights.

The woman/girl (*winking again and laughing*): Oh come on! It's not that high.

She leans over, grabs Pinky by his arm and pulls him toward herself. A struggle ensues. The woman/girl is persistent but Pinky is no less so. Besides he is stronger and the bedspread is slippery. Eventually the woman/girl winds up sliding off the bed, falling on top of him, and both of them sprawled intermixed on the floor, she laughing loudly and he trying not very successfully to match her.

Eventually they sit next to each other with their legs straight out breathing heavily.

The woman/girl (*turning her face to Pinky and winking at him once again with an impish look on her face*): Let's climb under the bed.

She sits closer to the bed and starts pulling Pinky in that direction.

Pinky immediately resists her as before. The prospect makes him shudder almost as much as the last proposal.

Pinky (*leaning the other way*): I ccccan't. I hhhhave cccclaustrophobia.

The woman/girl (*easing off, with surprise*): Really?

Pinky: Yeah. Rrrreal bbbbad.

The woman/girl (*serious*): I have claustrophobia too. But it's not too closed in under the bed for me. That's why I made them raise it. I love staying under beds. But I'm fine under this one. It's high enough. (*Changes the subject. Looking puzzled at Pinky.*) How come you're stuttering all of a sudden?

Pinky: It's bbbbecause I'm ssssitting ddddown. I ddddon't stttttutttter when I ssssstand up. That's why I ssssstand up mmmmost of the tttttime.

The woman/girl (*clapping her hands joyfully and laughing*): Oh it's cute. I love it. I wouldn't mind stuttering like that myself. Then I'd have to stand up all the time. It'd be fun. (*Goes back to the original subject.*) So you wouldn't feel comfortable under the bed?

Pinky: Nnnno I wwwwouldn't be for ssssure. I knnnnow thththhat. I ffffeel rrrreal uncomfortable in hhhigh and ccccclosed-in ppplaces. It's a rrrreal ppppproblem. (*Almost without a pause.*) Do you have a nnnneedle?

The woman/girl (*cheerfully*): I do.

She lets go of Pinky, pulls a needle out of the edge of her nightshirt/dress under her chin, and hands it to him.

The woman/girl (*cheerfully*): Here.

Pinky quickly grabs the needle and pricks the woman/girl with it high up on her arm where the sleeve ends.

She gives out a high-pitched shriek, looks at the place she has been pricked in, and covers it with her hand.

The woman/girl (*rubbing the spot and laughing*): Whew! It's fun. (*Reaches for the needle in Pinky's hand.*) Give it to me.

Pinky offers her the needle, she takes it, and quickly pricks Pinky on his upper arm through his shirt. Laughs.

Pinky yells, Ouch, laughs too, rubs the spot he has been pricked in, and reaches for the needle in the woman's/girl's hand.

She gives it to him willingly and he pricks her on her other arm in a similar spot.

She behaves as before, grabs the needle out of Pinky's hand, pricks him on his other arm in a similar spot, and the process is repeated a few times.

In the end they sit on the floor next to each other panting. It looks like they have had their fill of pricking each other. Their breathing gets gradually slower.

Pinky decides it is time for him to leave. He has accomplished everything he might have wanted and there is no point in his staying around.

Pinky *(still a little out of breath)*: I ggggguess I will lllleave nnnnow.

The woman/girl *(her breathing now almost normal)*: You're sure you don't want to rest a little... to catch your breath?

Pinky *(his breathing now almost normal too)*: Nnnno, I'm ffffine.... I will lllleave.

The woman/girl: Alright. *(After a pause.)* You know your way out.

Pinky *(gets up)*: Yes. *(After a pause.)* Right at the door, down the corridor, down the stairs, turn right, and out the front door.

The woman/girl: That's right. *(Changes the subject, amazed.)* You're right. You've stopped stuttering.... That's amazing.

Pinky *(relieved, smiling)*: Yeah.... I'm fine now. *(Goes back to the issue on his mind.)* And I turn left when I'm outside.

The woman/girl: Turn left. That's right. That's where you came from. I watched you coming in.

II. dirt and worms again

Pinky's dream.

He is alone in an orchard in the middle of the night. It is dark and cold. It is also windy. The trees are all leafless. It must be winter although it isn't frosty and there is no snow on the ground. He is kneeling down bent over. He is a little boy again, bare-legged and wearing shorts. The ground is soft under his knees. He reaches out with his hands and digs his fingers into the soil as if into the thick wool of a sheep. The sheep seems black. He has scooped up a bit of soil in each hand and brings both of them to his lips. He opens first one and shoves some of it into his mouth and then the other like a kid eating two apples at the same time wanting to make sure neither of them gets away. The soil is bland and doesn't taste bad. It reminds him of oatmeal porridge he eats every morning which he likes very much. He eats some more, alternating between the two hands. He presses his hands to his face when he has eaten up all loose soil and licks the dirt off with his tongue. He can feel it smeared over his face around his mouth and on his cheeks. The dirt feels sticky. He knows his face looks black now. There is something pleasant about the realization however.

He has eaten up all the soil in his hands and bends down to scoop up some more. When he digs his hands into the ground this time he feels something wiggling under the fingers of his right hand. It is an earthworm. He is overjoyed. He can have an earthworm this time. He grabs the earthworm in his fingers, pulls it out, straightens up, and looks at it. It is light enough in the garden for him to see it well. It is shiny and pinkish and struggles in his fingers trying to get away. It reminds him of the figure of Christ on a crucifix. He imagines Christ struggling like that on the cross when he was lifted up.

The worm looks juicy and appetizing. He tilts his head back, opens his mouth wide, and deposits it on his tongue. It writhes there as if on a hot skillet. This angers him because he hasn't done anything to it and he chomps down resolutely on it breaking it up into two or three pieces. Now it will know what being in trouble is!

The pieces keep wiggling desperately on their own and he chomps down on them once and then again and again, eventually chewing them up into a smooth lifeless paste. It is bland like the soil was earlier and also reminds him of the oatmeal porridge he eats every morning. He decides to swallow it, directs it with his tongue toward his gullet, gulps a couple of times, and feels it going down.

He remembers then that the worm had reminded him of Christ when he had pulled it out of the ground and recalls hearing or reading somewhere that in some churches they perform the rite of holy communion in which people are given little wafers to swallow which are told to represent symbolically the body of Christ. This is supposed to make them feel better and help them out in life. He concludes then that since to him the worm looked like Christ this is exactly what he is doing right now and that perhaps he is even closer to what is normally intended since the worm was pink like Christ's flesh had undoubtedly been. It is as if he were eating Christ's real body.

He closes his eyes and feels peace spread through him as he imagines happens to people who take part in holly communion and looks forward to a new, happier life.

12. pinky sees a church for the first time

Pinky trudged laboriously through the flat landscape. Clumps of the distance he had traveled clung to his feet making it hard for him to move forward. His past was unwilling to let him go.

Huge tracts of land, constituent parts of the landscape, rotated as he walked as if he traveled in a fast-moving train. An industrial-grade gray Formica sky hung low over the landscape.

At one point he came to a river. It was wide but shallow and fast-flowing and curved first this way then that, flaunting ostentatiously its unquestionable grace. The sandy flats in the bends it had created on their part proudly showed off the emptiness of their pristine white crescent shapes.

In one spot along the river women were doing their washing. Most of the time they stood bent down with their hands in the water but from time to time almost periodically would abruptly stand up and flap giant white sheets which they held in their hands—the linen they washed joined for an instant by the white in the air. These would billow voluptuously displaying for everyone to see the heretofore hidden aw-inspiring curvature of space.

Soap suds would gather about the women's legs in big white irregular shapes and from time to time again also essentially periodically pieces of these would break off and float down the river in the shape of wheels usually broken and sometimes completely smashed up.

Not too far downstream men—fishermen—were cleaning giant fish they had caught as big as hogs and the water ran red along that side of the river for a long way. The soapsuds would merge with it in places and the fish bladders that swam with the blood would mingle with the soap bubbles so that it was hard to tell one from the other.

After watching the two scenes for a while Pinky decided to move on and set off in his jerky laborious gait. He didn't have all the time in the world to dally around.

Eventually he found himself among trees. They grew thick in what appeared to be a sizeable wood and seemed to belong to some strange prehistoric species related to fishes because their crowns grew in one plane with the branches going off to the sides at an angle making them look like giant fish skeletons stoop upright. Their leaves had already all come off and densely carpeted the ground under them silver and rounded on one side like fish scales. Fall had already come to this part of the country. A little way back it was still summer.

It must have rained here recently too and heavily to boot for the dirt road that cut through the wood was all deep gooey mud. It stuck to Pinky's shoes even more than the distance/past earlier in his journey, bringing his progress nearly to a stand-still.

Still he pressed on.

The land grew gradually steeper and at one point a hill rose up in it like a giant malignant tumor under the skin.

Pinky's walking got excruciatingly difficult and he panted loudly, his raspy breath making his ears hurt.

Then suddenly he saw a sight he had never come across in his life—a thin shape rising from the ground skyward growing gradually thinner and thinner and ending in a dangerously sharp point at the end. It was the spire of a church.

He slowed down even more but forced himself to keep on walking. The shape kept rising higher and higher. (More and more of its bottom was revealing itself to him.) It was sticking so high up in the sky that its end could no longer be seen.

Eventually the roof the spire rose from came into view and Pinky guessed the edifice was most likely a church.

He found the spire astounding, stopped, and proceeded to trace its progress skyward with his eyes. In the end his head was horizontal in the back, parallel to the ground, and he felt himself falling backwards.

He didn't bother trying to break his fall and luckily landed on his back unhurt.

Still mesmerized he couldn't take his eyes off the magnificent shape.

Instinctively he spread his legs and arms wide and closing and opening the former and moving up and down the latter while thrashing with them hard on the ground traced out in the black mud the shape of an angel the same kind he used to make while trying to make one in fresh snow as a kid.

B. murtha

Pinky's dream.

It is a cold gloomy morning. It must be early spring or late fall. He is taking his usual Sunday morning walk. He is passing through a neighborhood he has never been in before. It is very much like all the other ones he has passed through on his walk however. It must therefore be in the same general area.

He is walking down the sidewalk. At this instant he is passing a little single-storied house on his left. It has a tall dark roof and is made from white clapboards. There is a door in the middle of the front wall and a window on each side of it. The door is painted a shiny black. It must be dark inside the house because the windows are black too. It seems they are on their own trying to match the color of the door.

There is a little garden in front of the hose. A black iron fence separates the garden from the street. A concrete path leads from the gate in the fence to the door.

Something grows right on the other side of the fence. The plants are tall. They look withered however and have fallen down in places. It must therefore be late fall rather than early spring.

He is curious about what the plants are. He stops, steps up to the fence, and looks.

The fence is tall and he has to look at the plants through the bars.

They have tall stalks with big flowers on the end. The flowers are cup-shaped and look more like tulips than roses. He decides they are roses however.

The flowers are charcoal gray and some near black. They also shine as if wet. He concludes it must have rained during the night and they are still wet from the rain.

The flowers look extremely sad. They look like human faces streaming with tears. He concludes the flowers are sad because they are about to die. He feels compassion for them and would like to help them.

Suddenly the flowers are no longer flowers but tiny emaciated human faces. They look like those of inmates behind barbed wire fences depicted in photographs of concentration camps. They stare at him with hope he might help them. He knows he can't do anything for them however. They will die no matter what he does. They are as good as dead already.

He looks up and sees there is a big chimney on top of the roof of the house. Somehow he hasn't noticed it before. Thick black smoke is billowing out of it skyward.

He becomes electrified. He grabs the bars of the fence and yells in the direction of the house at the top of his voice, Murtha! Murthaaaaaa! He doesn't know what the word Murtha means nor who he is calling to. Somehow it seems appropriate to do it however.

Immediately as on a stage the door of the house opens and a tall
and skinny old woman with white hair steps out. She wears a
dumpy old dress with a dirty apron over it and big worn slippers
on her feet.

He has never seen the woman before but feels as if he knows her
well. A warm feeling comes over him when he sees her.

He says to the woman, Do something with these flowers Murtha.
They can't be left standing like that.

Well, gather them up and carry them in, she says. We'll burn
them.

He had passed the gate in the fence already. He turns back, goes
inside the garden, closes the gate, and starts tearing the plants out
of the ground and putting them into a bundle which he presses to
his chest. They break easily as if not growing on woody stalks and
he doesn't have to pull them up by the roots. From time to time
he catches a glimpse of the flowers on the end of the stalks and
sees they look like tiny human faces but continues thinking of
them as plants. It is as if there were no difference between plants
and people. As he works he can feel the woman doing the same
next to him. She has come over to help him.

Soon they both have big bundles of the plants in their arms. It is hard for them to go on working. They stop ripping up the plants and walk to the house. Because he is carrying so much it is hard for him to see where he is going. He is doing his best however. The bundle is very light on the other hand and it is easy for him to carry it as if it were buoyant and were lifting him up. He thinks of the plants as shriveled up human corpses and it seems to be their nature that makes them rise up in the air like helium-filled balloons.

On coming out the woman has left the door open and the inside looks as black as the door itself did.

He goes first with the woman following him. He steps inside and stops. It is pitch black all around and he doesn't know which way to turn.

14. pinky goes to the cemetery

It was the eve of All Saints' Day and the weather had been engineered appropriately dramatic. The air was pitch-black and as Pinky's cheeks rubbed against it they would get smudged as if having brushed against a sooty wall. The sky was full of clouds and as the moon moved through them they would part before it in huge splashes like the sea before the bow of a ship. The bare tree branches made dry clanking sounds as they hit against each other testily in the strong wind. They were too close together. Bigger branches and tree trunks creaked with great effort complaining of the task they had been given. Mechanical owls set among the branches of the trees and (more often) on telephone poles made mournful hooting sounds imitating real ones. (Real owls had become extinct years ago.)

Pinky trudged along in his habitual laborious gait leaning forward and stomping his feet down hard on the ground as always encased in heavy mountain climber's boots as if trying to squash something detestable under them (cockroaches or worms) or (or perhaps and) wanting to leave deep imprints everywhere he treaded as a proof of his existence.

As he neared the edge of the town he passed the tall tenement buildings on his right and left standing completely dark with not a light in any of the windows as if filled with concrete from top to bottom. He was seeing them for the last time.

The temporary wooden bridge sounded hollow under his feet as he was crossing it. He was hearing the sounds it made also for the last time. His feet would never tread it again. He put them down especially hard, much harder than before, and enjoyed the booming noise they made. They were grateful to him for making them sound so loud and were doing their best to fulfill his wish while cheering him on at the same time.

Beyond the bridge the progress got more difficult. He no longer could see anything. He let his feet find the road on their own as it labored up the hill.

At one point he stumbled on something and nearly fell down. It was a spade with a long handle which someone has left in the middle of the road. He picked it up and carried it along. It wasn't excluded that he would need it.

Eventually he discerned the outline of the cemetery at the top of the hill—its tall white wall and the tree tops like boys' unruly hair sticking out from behind it. The only issue now was how to find the gate.

He found it without looking for it. It must have waited for him and came by itself.

Inside there was not a soul—that is body—in sight. The atmosphere was festive. Lights flickered on the graves and the ground had been swept clean. In places it even glittered like a new parquet floor. He had been told his mother's grave was there somewhere but he had no time to look for it just then. He would do it some other time. He had to attend to his own first.

He had never seen it before but knew where it was—fifteen steps ahead, eleven to the left, three to the right, turn left, and there it was.

It had a masonry parapet on its one shorter and two longer sides and steps going down as if into a subway.

At the bottom there was a thin sliver—faint smudge—of light. The door had been left ajar. Soft music was streaming from the inside. It was wonderful—they had not only left the light on for him but had put a record on the player!

your childhood

Tu infancia en Mentón

Federico García Lorca

I. they are flying kites

It was late spring or perhaps early fall and Franz was out on the plain outside Blutburg, the city he lived in. The ground under his feet was hard consisting of red clay, gravel, and sand and totally barren. There was no tree, blade of grass, or any other kind of vegetation to be seen anywhere as far as the eye could see. The land was so flat you could notice the curvature of the earth and even feel it with the soles of your feet. Franz was afraid of falling down, rolling all the way to the horizon, and disappearing behind it and he was constantly digging the sides of his shoes into the ground to prevent that from happening.

He wore short tight black pants that reached below his knees and a dirty white long-sleeved shirt with the buttons on both of the cuffs missing. On his feet he wore high-topped brown shoes without any socks. The leather in the shoes was hard from having been wet many times and felt like iron. From their appearance the shoes indeed seemed to be made from sheet iron rusty and dented in spots and looked very uncomfortable. It seemed certain the feet in them must be badly chafed. The shoelaces in both shoes were torn and tied by knots in places. The knots stuck up above the shoes like disheveled hair on top of a person's head.

The pockets in Franz's pants were stuffed with rocks which he carried to defend himself with in case he was attacked by someone. He also carried a heavy stick to defend himself with when he had to. He had stained one end of it—the heavier one—with blood to scare off any potential attackers. He had managed to sneak into the slaughterhouse yard, dip the stick in the puddle of blood left over from a recently slaughtered steer, and get away before being caught. This was a few weeks ago and the blood had turned brown but you could tell what it was. Franz carried the stick by its thinner end letting the heavier one drag on the ground. He didn't feel like exerting extra energy by carrying the stick in the air.

There was no one around and Franz didn't feel there was any imminent danger of him being attacked. He therefore felt relaxed. He had wandered off from the city to be away from potential attackers in order to relax. It was hard to stay that way in town. He felt good.

The town of Blutburg could be seen in the distance like an enormous pile of bloodstained bandages stacked up haphazardly in the middle of the plain—three- and four-storied tenement buildings and medieval houses with steep tiled roofs, behind a wall, the white in them the lime and the red the clay which was the chief ingredient in the material from which everything in the town was built.   Hence the name "Blutburg"—"Blood Fortress/Town."

The sky was a faded blue and perfectly clear. It was daytime, late morning or early afternoon, and appropriately bright, but Franz didn't cast any shadow and the sun was nowhere to be seen as if it had wandered off somewhere unauthorized taking with itself its shadow-casting ability but not its light.

Franz had been walking around with his head bent down to see if he would find something valuable on the ground but as he accidentally looked up at one point he saw the most beautiful sight he had ever seen—a huge, long-tailed kite, all the colors of the rainbow, fluttering high up above him. It bobbed up and down and darted from side to side having a time of its life unaware of and/or uncaring about the miserable land below. Until then Franz had no idea anything so beautiful existed. He had seen a kite or two before but they were puny affairs pathetic in their attempts at something they clearly weren't up to. Now he couldn't take his eyes off the kite. It was big and beautiful, looking as it should and capable of doing everything that could be expected of a kite. Who was flying it? Whom did it belong to?

Unaware of what he was doing, his head still thrown back and the stick in his hand dragging on the ground, he began walking in the direction where the kite was being flown from. He couldn't see the string it was flying on—it was too thin for that—but had little doubt where it was being held—the direction opposite to where the tail was pointing which was the town.

He kept on walking without taking his eyes off the kite, nearly losing his balance from time to time, the heavy stick scraping the ground. The kite seemed to follow him. It was so high up that no matter where he was it seemed to be directly above him. It fluttered and darted from side to side drunk with its beauty and freedom.

Even though he didn't take his eyes off the kite Franz could see with the lower edge of his vision he was nearing the town. The main gate was a little to the right of where he had been heading to so he adjusted his course. His neck hurt from being thrown back for so long but Franz didn't want to do anything which might make him lose the sight of the kite even for an instant. He would suffer for as long as he had too.

The kite clearly wasn't being flown from the closer side of the town and probably not from the center. Was it from the far side? From outside the walls beyond? And if so then how far beyond the walls? The far side of the horizon? Then he might never get there and find out who was flying it.

A stab of pain pierced his heart at the prospect of this happening but he pressed on. He wouldn't let himself lose hope and would do everything he could to find out who was flying the kite.

He passed through the gate and entered the town. Now he would lose sight of the kite from time to time when a chimney, roof, or wall would shield it from his eyes but would find it a moment later. The kite also was no longer above his head but further back. He had to bend his neck more and at times turn around and walk backwards in order to see it.

He walked down the main street cutting through the town and then through the central square.

People would laugh at him saying, Did you lose something up there? He went the other way! or things like that. Franz paid no attention to them and kept on walking. He followed the main street on the other side of the square. At one point he noticed he was no longer holding the stick in his hand. He had dropped it unawares. It didn't matter. He pressed on.

He still couldn't see the string and couldn't tell where the kite was flown from but it was a long way off. Yet he still couldn't tell if it was in the town itself or outside it.

He envisioned now who was flying it—a beautiful young girl with long flaxen hair, cornflower eyes, and a porcelain face, dressed in a blue velvet dress trimmed with golden piping. She wore white stockings and on her feet little gold slippers. Next to her helping her fly the kite stood her father—tall and handsome, with long golden hair, a similar short beard, and sparkling blue eyes, dressed in a dark green velvet suit and tall yellow boots. He had been traveling in foreign lands and had bought the kite in a beautiful white city to give it to his daughter. He had come back the night before and was now showing it to her. The image was so vivid Franz felt he saw it with his eyes.

He kept on walking. The edge of the town was nearing. Would he have to cross the gate? How far beyond the wall would he have to go? Will he ever get to the man and the girl? Suddenly he was sure he wouldn't. He never got anything he really craved. His heart was up in his throat throbbing so loud he could barely hear his footsteps. Still he kept on walking.

The sharp triangle of a red roof suddenly swallowed up the kite. Did he lose it for good? His heart sank and the world went still. But then the kite emerged as beautiful and lively as before and with it like a thin crease in the faded fabric of the sky the string it was flying on.

Joy like a scream burst out inside him. The string went steeply down into the thicket of roofs just ahead of him. This is where he lived! His house was just around the corner. Was the kite being flown from it? Just as he had been sure he would never see the beautiful girl and her father before now he was certain he would. He imagined them standing at the doorstep of his house jointly holding the string the kite flew on, welcoming him with smiles on their faces.

He rushed frantically to where the string descended. There was a little narrow side street just up ahead on his left. He turned into it. The string went further down on the right. He took the next alley in that direction. The string went down a few houses further on the left. This wasn't where his house stood but at this point it didn't matter. It was close enough. In a matter of seconds he would be there! He ran into the passage between the buildings and found himself in a courtyard full of stacks of wood and barrels—barely begun, half-done, and finished. This is where the cooper Meyer lived, which was just across the wall from his house. The string went steeply down into the courtyard like a stone plunging.

Wet with sweat and panting Franz stopped with his mouth wide open and looked up.

Like a bird the string swooped down from the sky and gently settled in the stubby sausage fingers of the cooper Meyer who sat in a chair on the second floor porch looking up. His big round face shone like a loaf of freshly baked bread and his wide thin mouth was open and shaped into a big black O. He wore his favorite worn mustard-brown army jacket, way too tight for him now, held together high up on his chest by two tin buttons that threatened to pop off. It was open under the chin and his neck bulged out of its collar red with blood and covered with swollen veins. Below, his belly stuck out from between the two sides of the coat like the back of a fat pig hiding under his shirt. His forearms rested comfortably on it—it was easier for him to hold them up this way.

On his left closer to Franz stood his ten-year old idiot daughter Gretel dressed also in her favorite faded flowered dress with a big white bib under her chin stained as always with porridge and gravy the straw-colored hair on her pointed head tied in two frayed braids. She was also looking up when Franz appeared and drooled from her open mouth but noticed Franz instantly, looked at him with her milky eyes, and thrusting her index finger up into the sky exclaimed excitedly, Huh, huh, huh! She had always been crazy about him.

2. blutball

For the rest of his life Franz was to remember that late spring afternoon (or rather early spring evening) when he was with his father in the kitchen of their apartment and the latter was making the deathbed. The kitchen was a perfect cube, the height of its walls equal to their width and therefore with an unusually high ceiling, which made anyone inside it feel vulnerable. The coarse-grained walls in the color of which predominated the blue-gray of cement were bare and tinged in just the right places with the green-gray stains of mold to make them look gloomier. To add to the atmosphere all of the furniture had been taken out of the room and the only item that remained (actually it wasn't an item of furniture but an inseparable part of the room) was the built-in masonry stove in the corner near the door. There actually was a true item of furniture in the room at the moment which was a three-legged wooden stool normally used by Franz's father in his everyday work. (He was a cobbler.) It had been brought in by Franz and stood in the corner of the room under the only window. The window was very high up almost under the ceiling and it was difficult even for an adult to look out through it while standing on the floor. Franz stood on his toes on top of the stool so that he could see the outside better. The frame had also been taken out of the window for a stronger effect and what remained was an empty square hole which went well with the empty space inside. The setting sun cast its wan light through it into a corner under the ceiling like a giant spider hastily weaving its cobweb for the night.

Franz's father worked in the corner opposite to where Franz stood. Even though a cobbler he was handy with the saw, hammer, and nails, earning an odd mark here and there as a carpenter or cabinet maker, and had decided to build himself that item of furniture which is indispensable in every family. He had been postponing making it for years and luckily it hadn't been needed but things couldn't go on being good forever. Sooner or later its lack would be felt.

He was working with pine boards white as paper and light (not heavy) as was clear from the way he handled them and it looked as if they weren't wooden boards but three-dimensional objects made from white paper glued together to look like boards. The bed grew slowly but steadily in the corner on the floor like another spider web, a companion to the one in the opposite corner under the ceiling. It seemed its unusual complex shape had to do with its ultimate use which had nothing to do with joy.

Looking out the window Franz could see the flat bare plain outside the town stretching to the horizon. The ground was red, covered with sharp rocks. The sun was low although not visible and the rocks cast long shadows that looked like tears in black clothing hanging loose. Not far away boys were playing the game of *Steinball* (stone ball) also known as *Blutball* (blood ball). It consisted of the players of one team hitting with sticks rocks in the direction of those of the second one and those of the second one blocking the rocks with their bodies or hitting them back with sticks which the players of the first team then had to block or hit in return. Hitting a rock back with a stick gave you a point. Catching a rock with your hand counted for extra. Blocking one with your head counted for more. Catching it in your mouth counted the most.

The boys were dressed for the most part in white shirts open all the way down to the waist (catching the stone in your shirt also got you extra points), tight black pants that reached to below the knee, and high-topped shoes worn over bare feet the color of rusty iron and shaped like rusty iron sheets twisted so that they looked like leather.

Incredible blood-curdling screams the boys made punctuated the still air amidst dry cracking of rocks being hit by sticks. In a few places bodies—half white and half black—lay on the ground, limp and motionless with their arms and legs spread out casting shadows like huge tears in black clothing. In some cases patches of red color huddled against the bodies reluctant to stray away into the open—blood stains on the clothing or puddles of blood on the ground.

3. scabs

Hier kommt der grosse Franz mit seinem kleinen Schwanz (Here comes big Franz with his little tail [=penis]), Gert said quietly as Franz approached him. His red hair caked with dry sweat shone and curled up at the ends as if soaked in varnish. Virulent brown freckles like specks made by flies suffering from bloody diarrhea clustered thick around his eyes and nose. The hole in place of his missing two front teeth stuck out over his lower lip like black buck teeth.

Da steht der kleine Gert mit seinem riesigen Schwert (There stands little Gert with his giant sword [=penis]), Franz answered barely audibly seeing his friend's scrawny figure grow big with his every step as the latter leaned with his shoulder against the broad square stone pillar. The shadow of the arches reflected in the wet stone slabs skipped off into the distance behind him like echoes of a loud O.

When he was close enough Franz swung the heavy stick he carried in his right hand at Gert's head but the latter deflected it nimbly with his stick which he held in his left one, swung it around, and let it fly at Franz. It almost hit Franz on the head but he was quick enough to duck to his right so that the stick merely grazed the top of his left arm and slid to the ground. Nonetheless it left a dull pain in his shoulder which stuck there like a clump of dirt. The stick crashed loudly on the ground next to Franz's foot sending off a series of echoes which chased off after the reflections of the arches.

Franz swung his stick back at his friend's ribs but his feet slid under him on the wet surface and he came crashing down on his left hip and elbow. Once down however he swung his stick again at the Gert's left leg and caught him just below the knee. The latter yelped like a puppy, let the stick fall out of his hand, clutched the spot that had just been hit, and fell to the ground on his right side. He stayed there, leaning on his right elbow and massaging the back of his leg with his left hand. The two boys faced each other like funereal terra cotta figures in an Etruscan tomb.

The spot on his left hip where Franz had landed hurt but he refused to acknowledge the pain shifting his attention to the cold that streamed from the stone into his body along the side of his left leg and the arm on which he was resting.

The stone's warm, he said causally, looking at Gert.

Hot, Gert said stirring on the hard surface as if in soft bed.

Franz stirred too and started getting up. Gert followed him. He made a face as he put his weight on his left foot but caught himself immediately and the grimace vanished before it had time to fully form. They picked up their sticks and stepped up to each other.

Schweinhund/Scheissdreck (Pig dog/shit mud), they exchanged greetings as they shook hands. Silently they strode around the massive pillar and walked side by side in Franz's original direction, Gert on Franz's left. The feeling of pain and cold faded in Franz's memory as if left behind on the ground where he had lain. His stomach gurgled—he hadn't had anything to eat yet that morning.

Instinctively he turned his head left and noticed Gert was munching on something.

What are you shitting [=eating]? He asked.

Without saying a word, continuing to munch, Gert stuck his hand in his pocket, pulled something out, and extended his fist to Franz. Franz reached out with his hand, opened it, and felt something dry and light trickle into his palm nearly filling it in the end. It was *Schörfe* (scabs) also known as *Bluterbsen* (blood peas)—drops of pig blood dripped onto a hot stove which turned into hard, irregularly shaped flakes you ate. They were among his favorite things to munch on. He was hoping this is what Gert was eating when he asked the question. Gert's father knew someone at the slaughterhouse and from time to time was regaled by the person with a pitcher of fresh blood. Gert's mother would make these for breakfast. They never had them at Franz's home.

Franz cupped his hand so as not to spill any of the precious things, brought his hand close to his mouth, and skillfully scooped some flakes up with his lips like a horse. His tongue directed them inside his mouth, they found their way between his teeth, were ground up there, and mixing with saliva released their delicate sweet flavor. As always it evoked in Franz's mind the beautiful image of blood spreading in water.

He chewed up all of the flakes, let them dissolve as much as possible in his saliva, and swallowed the lot. Then he scooped up another bunch, carefully guarding the rest in his hand so as not to spill even a single one. A sense of wellbeing spread through his body. He couldn't think of anything else he might want. The sound of their footsteps on the hard stone slabs echoed in unison and from time to time his shoulder touched that of his friend. The shadow of the arches skipped along before them disappearing in the distance. Suddenly, as if on command, they both started humming the ditty which was the current rage among the boys in town:

Meine liebe Karoline
Zeig mir deine Fickmaschine!

(My darling Caroline
Show me your fuck machine!)

4. milk

The rain fell steadily onto the gray cobblestones as if into another sky—from the empty sky above into the stone sky below. The thin film of water covering the stones trembled with each drop as if shivering with cold. Franz stood arching his shoulders forward to lessen the area of contact between his back and the wall against which he pressed as hard as he could to keep himself out of the rain. The warmth was flowing out of his body into the cold stone as if through a funnel. The street was empty and you could only hear the lisping whisper of the raindrops as they hit the ground.

Suddenly a rhythmic sound could be heard coming from around the corner on his left—clap-clap, clap-clap—wooden clogs moving down the stone sidewalk. Beate was coming!

Franz stuck his head out while bending a little to decrease the chance of being noticed and saw her walking toward him some hundred feet away tall and slender in her long dark dress, the big metal can in her left hand adding to her tallness by almost reaching the ground.

He ducked back instantly but she obviously had seen him because she stopped upon coming around the corner and turned right to face him.

What are you doing here? She asked.

Waiting for you, he answered turning to face her, now pressing his left side to the wall.

Why? She insisted, her face smoothing out in the direction of a smile although she stopped it from going all the way. It was clear she knew what was going on and was playing a game.

So that you'd let me drink, he answered obediently, playing along.

Drink what? She asked, finally smiling, unable to keep her face from misbehaving.

Milk, he said seriously unable to stop himself from playing her game.

Milk? She said in turn, raising her voice, the smile vanishing from her face and being replaced by a stern expression bordering on anger. Why, I just let you have some milk a couple of days ago. What do you think I am—your milkmaid?

But I'm hungry, he pleaded with despair in his voice, as if truly forgetting they were playing a game. I haven't had anything to eat yet today.

Why doesn't your mother give you some milk? She asked.

She's sick, he answered. And besides we don't have any money to buy milk.

She didn't say anything at first and gave a big sigh, screwing up her face, but then added reluctantly, Alright, just a little.... But it's the last time. Do you hear?

He said nothing, glad the game was finally over and that it would be played again in a few days, and stepped up to her as she put the can down on the ground and took the lid off it with her right hand.

He knelt down obediently as if in church during communion but instead of throwing his head back bent it down to reach for the can.

She tilted it forward with her free hand and he saw the round bluish disk of milk inside it rise on the near side toward him and sensed the sweet warm vapor caress his face.

He bent down further, she tilted the can some more, he closed his eyes, touched the thick, cold edge of the can with his teeth, stuck his upper lip out until it joined the warm liquid, sucked, felt the sweet current flow into his mouth, and swallowed. Peace like warmth spread through his consciousness. He sucked more, swallowed, repeated the process, and then repeated it again and again. He did it some dozen times until he heard her say, It's enough now. Stop it! You'll drink the whole can!, and then tilt the can away from him.

He didn't protest but again obediently moved his lips away, leaned back, and stood up.

Warmth and wetness persisted on his upper lip even as he was standing and he wiped it off with the back of his hand, smearing the liquid around his mouth so that for a few seconds it seemed to have lost its shape. The cold brought everything back to normal after a few seconds.

She put the lid back on, straightened up, and lifted the can. Her black hair was pushing its way out from under the white kerchief tied tightly around her head in little round curls like carving in a statue on the façade of a church. Another instant and she would be gone. The prospect frightened him.

Then an idea flashed through his mind and he realized it had been there all along except he hadn't let it come to the surface.

Let me see it, he said with fear seizing his throat like a bony hand. He almost choked.

See what? She asked earnestly, apparently not understanding him.

It, he said, his throat dry, and jabbed with his finger in the direction of her abdomen.

Whaaat? She asked incredulously, her face dissolving in laughter. It?... Are you crazy?

But you showed it to me last week, he said emboldened, his fear gradually replaced by a confidence encouraged by her behavior. Show it to me again.

No, she said sternly, I told you it was just that one time, and his confidence that had fully formed itself by then vanished in an instant like a soap bubble bursting and was replaced by deep gloom.

But Beatchen, please, he pleaded passionately, using the endearing form of her name. Just once more. I promise I won't ask for it again.

No, she again said sternly. I shouldn't have shown it to you before. Now you'll want me to show it to you every day.

No, no, I promise, I won't, he shouted desperately as if his life depended on what he was asking. I'll pay you, he blurted out at the last moment, remembering he had a coin in his pocket. He stuck his hand into it, took the coin out, and extended it to her.

Take it, he said.

No, she said firmly but then unexpectedly asked, How much do you have?

Five pfennigs, he said.

Five pfennigs?! She burst out laughing. You want me to show it to you for five pfennigs?!... Her dark eyes flashed like daggers.

But that's all I have, he said barely audibly, ashamed, letting his hand drop.

No, she answered firmly, but than unexpectedly stuck her hand out and said, Let me see it.

Not understanding what that meant he mechanically stuck his hand out and let her take the coin.

She looked at it, said, Alright, but just this time, and put the can down on the ground again.

He still didn't believe this would happen, but she brought her hands down, took the skirt of her dress in her fingers, and raised it high above her waist, her hands almost up to her chin.

For an instant he thought he had fainted and everything had gone white. It was the whiteness of her skin contrasting with the dark of the skirt above, in the back, and on the sides that overwhelmed him. Her belly was round and the full thighs grew naturally out of it branching more and more apart as they went downward. They ended in disproportionately thin legs which in turn ended in disproportionately small feet that looked out of place in the big clunky clogs. A big clump of black unruly hair stuck out arrogantly from between her thighs where they met as if she carried a whole lot more of it there, trying to divert his attention away from her skin. He disregarded it however as if considering it not to be part of her like a dirt mark easily washed off by water or an object out of place capable of being swept away by a casual swipe of the hand.

Mesmerized, his consciousness a never-ending white, he stood with his eyes wide open and mouth ajar unaware of time and place.

Then unexpectedly she said, That's enough, let the skirt out of her finger, and it dropped, wiping the image out as off a blackboard.

Franz jerked and blinked as if waking up. He realized then what had happened and wanted to protest but knew he had no right to do that. He had gotten much more than had had expected and deserved. The disappointment persisted in him however like a rock chafing in a shoe.

She lifted up the can, looked provocatively into his eyes with a curl of a smile on her lips, and turning left threw the coin he had given her at his feet. It made a pitiful pinging sound as it hit the ground.

She proceeded in her original direction and in a few strides hid behind the corner of the house on the other side of the street.

Da geht die Beate mit seiner Fotzgranate (There goes Beate with her cunt grenade), the phrase started to form itself mechanically in his mind as he watched her walk away but he quashed it instantly so that it didn't have time to develop fully.

5. a passion play

The play was conceived, planned out, and performed largely by Gert. It took place in the basement of his house. The room was square with a small window under the ceiling on the street side of the house. From time to time during the performance people would walk one way or the other past the window and the shadow of their legs would darken the already dimly lit space.

Sacks full of coal were piled up against one wall arranged in such a way that the shorter ones were on the sides and the taller ones in the middle. They were to represent Golgotha. The sacks were all closed except for the one in the very middle which was open. It was packed full with lumps of coal to make it easier to stand up the crosses in them.

The crosses were made from sticks and held together with nails. The bigger one, which was more than twice as big as the other two, was meant for the figure of Christ and the two smaller ones for those of the robbers. The first was to be played by a rat and the second by two mice. All three were caught the night before and held in separate jars—the rat in a big one and the two mice in a smaller one.

Against the wall opposite to those with the sacks stood the chorus—four girls and three boys. It didn't include Gert, Franz, and two other boys who helped in the performance. The chorus was dressed in old sacks folded in such a way that they could be worn as capes with hoods. This is the way Gert thought the inhabitants of Palestine dressed in the old times. Gert, Franz, and the other two boys were dressed in their normal clothes but the last two held tall sticks in their hands. They played the roles of Roman soldiers.

When everything was readied and the chorus stood still Gert got the jar with the mice from the corner where it had stood all night and brought it to the middle of the pile of sacks. The three crosses, twine, knife, hammer and some nails were already laid out there.

Gert stuck his hand into the jar with the mice, grabbed one as it huddled against its companion, and with Franz and one of the two boys helping, tied it to one of the two smaller crosses with a piece of twine. Its paws were too short to support it on the cross, so he wrapped its body tightly with the twine and fastened it firmly to the stick. The mouse made a few squeals while being fastened but it didn't present any real difficulty. The second mouse was fastened to the cross in the same way. It squealed a little more but otherwise also wasn't a problem. The two crosses were stood up in the middle sack, one on each edge of it, leaving room for the big cross between them.

The rat was a different matter. When Gert tried to take it out of the jar it bit his finger. Gert let out a scream and cursed loudly and sucked the blood out of the wound not sure how to proceed. Franz suggested he wrap his hand in a rag but Gert thought it would make it too difficult for him to grab the rat so he quickly stuck his hand in the jar and grabbed the rat by its neck. It squealed like a stuck pig and tried to wiggle itself out of Gert's hand. At one point it twisted its body so much it nearly managed to bite Gert again. Furious, he smashed it down on a sack while holding it tight and as that didn't quiet the rat he did it a few more times until it stopped squirming. The rat had been apparently hurt and stayed still with its mouth open and panting.

Fastening the rat to the cross proved also difficult. It regained its strength, squealed, and wiggled again, managing even to bite Franz on one of his fingers. The bite wasn't nearly as bad as Gert's and it hardly bled at all.

Nailing the rat through its paws proved impossible however—they were too small. As a consequence the rat was tied to the cross the same way as the two mice. But then Gert got a big nail and drove it all the way through the rat's belly so that it stuck out in the back. The rat didn't squeal this time and didn't appear to squirm perhaps because it was tied too tight. It opened its mouth very wide however and panted rapidly like a dog.

The cross was stood up in the middle of the sack and the rat hung on it, its tail drooping down and trailing on top of the coal. It glared fiercely at the figures before him however panting furiously with its mouth wide open, ready to bite. Its small white teeth stood out frighteningly sharp against the bright red mouth.

The chorus had tried to come up closer to the sacks to see better what was being done on two occasions, first when the first mouse was being tied to the cross and then when they were tying down the rat but Gert had shooed them away and they remained standing obediently against the wall.

Having finished with the rat Gert made his three helpers stand back too and while facing the crucifixion scene began singing in his cracking voice the hymn they all knew, *Erkenne mich mein Hüter* (Take note of me my keeper). Everyone joined in and it was sung to the end.

When they had finished they tried to think of another hymn but when they couldn't agree on one someone started up, *O, Tannenbaum!* (Oh, Christmas tree!) and it was instantly picked up by everyone and sung with vigor to the end.

Silence fell over the room when the carol was finished. Everyone stood still looking at the crucifixion scene. The two mice didn't stir and seemed asleep, comfortable in their cocoons of twine as if under featherbeds. Their thin tails hung limply down onto the coal. The rat still panted however with its mouth wide open as if threatening those that had harmed it with its sharp white teeth. Blood had collected inside its mouth and gleamed in one of its corners red like a ruby.

He's still alive! Someone shouted.

He wants to bite us! Shouted someone else.

Kill him! Screamed a third voice.

Kill him! Kill him! everyone shouted and Gert then rushed forward, grabbed a big lump of coal from the top of the sack, and hit the rat with it, knocking over the cross.

Everyone ran over to the sacks, fists flew, some empty and some with lumps of coal in them, and in a matter of seconds the scene on top of the sack was reduced to shambles. The crosses were smashed and the animals turned into tattered bloody rags. Gert hit with his lump of coal what was left over of the rat a few more times and then once each those of the mice, and finally threw the lump on top of the sack. He turned and looked with pride at the other kids.

Someone applauded and then everyone joined in, including Gert.

When the applause ceased, Gert faced the sacks, fell on his knees, and started reciting the Lord's Prayer. Everyone obediently did the same. The voices resounded hollow in the largely empty space like in a classroom. When they had finished, everyone spontaneously proceeded with Hail Mary without the trace of a pause.

6. black milk

Franz is in an empty room. It appears to be a cube. There is no light in the room and no windows visible and it is dark but light enough for him to see. It might be a room in a basement with a window under the ceiling behind his back. He is on his knees facing a corner. On the ground in the corner there stands a strange black triangular dish fitting tightly into it. It is glazed and shines even in the half-darkness. A tall female figure wearing a long dark dress stands near the corner against the wall on his right bending down and holding a pitcher made of similar black glazed clay. She is about to pour something into the dish. He doesn't know who the person is except that it is a young woman. She will be pouring milk for him to drink.

The woman tips the pitcher and black liquid flows in a thin stream from its spout into the dish. This doesn't disturb him. Even though the liquid is black it is still milk. Milk apparently can be black or white. He bends down and tries to drink from the dish but can't do it because his forehead presses against the two walls. The dish is too small.

He presses harder and bends down lower and after straining for a while manages to touch the edge of the dish with his lips. He presses some more and now can reach the milk. He has managed to push the walls away. But the dish has also gotten bigger. Now it sticks way out of the corner.

He tries to sucks on the milk but there is very little of it in the dish. His lips right away touch its bottom. The woman notices this and pours more milk into the dish closer to the corner so that she misses his hair. She can do that easily since the dish has gotten bigger.

The level of the milk in the dish rises and he starts sucking again. It is easier for him to drink on the edge of the dish with his lower lip against it and the upper inside. The milk now flows plentiful into his mouth. It is cold and has no taste but he is satisfied with it. He didn't expect anything else. This is what black milk should taste like. The woman keeps pouring the milk and he keeps drinking it.

Then he notices something is tickling his lower lip. It is short curly hair. It apparently grows out of the edge of the dish. It must have been there all along but he merely hadn't noticed it. This was probably because the hair grows sparse. The black glazed surface of the dish was apparently shining through it as the skull of a man with his hair thinning on top.

The hair doesn't bother him and he keeps on sucking the milk in. In fact he likes the hair being there. It tickles his lip in a pleasant way and besides it prevents anything that might be in the milk from getting inside his mouth. It serves as a strainer.

The woman keeps on pouring the milk and even though he keeps on drinking it its level in the dish rises. He has to suck more because the milk will spill over onto the floor. He keeps doing it but there is more and more of the milk coming. He is afraid he will choke. He has to tell the woman to ease off.

He raises his head so as to speak to her and sees her tower over him with the pitcher in her hand, the black stream coming out of its spout steady like a shiny metal rod. Seeing what he has done however the woman moves the pitcher over and pours the milk on his face. It spills all over it and he has to close his eyes.

She has done it as a joke for he can hear her laugh. She doesn't stop at this however but keeps on pouring the milk. He wants to tell her to stop and opens his mouth but she pours the milk straight into it. He nearly chokes, wants to shout for her to stop, but is afraid he will drown, so he swallows the milk. She keeps on pouring it and he keeps on swallowing.

He hopes she will pause for a second so that he can tell her to stop what she is doing but she goes on and on. There apparently will be no end to it—the pitcher is bottomless. He cannot drink so much so fast. Eventually he will choke. Then it happens. The liquid goes down into his lungs and he can't breathe. In despair he coughs and tries to scream. At that instant he wakes up.

7. the performance

Franz leaned against the square pillar wishing for the two shadows to merge. He preferred being part of the darkness under the arcades rather than of the light in the square.

A throng of people filled the center of the square tightly packed like a swarm of bees. In the very middle of the square stood a tall round structure made of wood sloping on the sides and flat in the middle with a white chair in the center. The wood was new and could have been called white if it weren't for the snow-white chair. It was yellow in comparison. Bright white light coming from some unknown source illuminated the structure.

A tiny white figure, the same shade as the chair, appeared on top of the structure and walked to the chair. It was dressed in a loose white shirt and pants and its skin was all white too, nearly the same color as the clothes. Its head was completely bald and shone like a billiard ball. The figure—a little man—carried something in its hands, clutching it to its body, wide and rounded at the ends and pinched in the middle. The object was bright red and looked like the bloody body of a woman.

Did the little man kill the woman and was being punished for that? Was he going to be burned on top of the pile of wood together with the body after being tied down to the chair? Franz's heart pounded loud in his ears so that he had trouble hearing. He felt weak in the knees and leaned harder on the pillar to stay up. But his eyesight went dark and he passed out.

When he came to he was lying down on the ground his cheek on a cobblestone but no longer by the pillar except out in the square just behind the outer ring of the people filling it. He had crawled forward while unconscious.

His fear was gone, replaced by a curiosity of how the burning was going to happen. From his position he could see nothing. He got up and pushed his way in among the people.

He still couldn't see anything so he proceeded pushing his way forward. He was like water forcing its way through a pile of rocks.

Nobody objected to his pushing his way through and soon he found himself close to the inside edge of the crowd. There were just a few people ahead of him and he decided to force his way all the way forward to where a bunch of kids and old men stood in a curving line. In a few seconds he was there. There was nothing now between him and the structure and it stood just a few feet before him blinding-white in the strong light.

It was not made from logs as he had thought but from boards which were nailed down close to each other. The little man for some reason was bending over the chair with his back toward him. He turned around, sat down in the chair, and Franz saw it was not a man but a boy about the same age as he except smaller, completely hairless, and with milk-white skin. The red thing he held in his hands was not the body of a woman but an object that looked like a huge violin—a woman-violin, he thought of it. It was the same size as the boy and seemed light because the boy handled it with ease. It rested on a spindle between the boy's feet while he held it by the neck with his right hand. In his left hand he held a bow the same color as the woman-violin which he must have carried all along but which couldn't be seen from afar.

The boy's head was bent down and deep furrows ran along his white forehead like ripples on the surface of milk. His eyes were closed. Suddenly he threw his head back, lifted the bow in his left hand, hit the strings with it, and it was as if he had sunk a knife into a living being. The woman-violin was alive! She gave out a loud moan of unbearable pain. The boy didn't pay attention to it but still keeping his head back and his eyes closed continued moving the bow back and forth over the strings making the woman-violin sigh, sob, moan and scream with pain. The sounds filled the whole square and covered the people crowding in it.

Franz stood petrified. He had never heard or imagined anything similar. He didn't know what he was hearing but was overwhelmed by it. He stood without moving for what seemed a long time aware only of the sounds and only gradually grew conscious of himself and his surroundings. People around him stood still as he, affected by the sounds apparently in the same way, and he could hear strange sniffling from around and behind him. It sounded like people were suffering from colds. Then he sniffled himself and realized tears were running down his cheeks— he like the people in the crowd was crying.

How long was this going to continue? He wondered. When was the boy going to be burned?

Eventually, unable to stand the tension, after giving a big sniff and wiping his face with his hand, he tugged at the sleeve of the old man next to him. When are they going to burn him? He asked as the man bent down.

The man said nothing at first but then pressed his index finger to his lips, saying, Shhhh. Later, later, he added in a whisper while straightening up.

8. the rehearsal

This time there wasn't a soul in the square. The strong sunlight chased the arches on one side of it and they tried to evade it by leaning back their shadows.

It was stifling hot and that was probably why the boy had set the chair out in the passageway in front of the door of the hotel to do his practicing. Sunlight did fall on his feet but the rest of him was hidden in the shadow cast by the arch and out in the passageway the air was at least stirring. In his room it was probably dead still as putrid water in a pond.

He was dressed in the same clothes as the night before and sat in the same kind of chair but the woman-violin was different—white instead of red, the same color as the chair.

Franz hid behind the pillar as much as he could while trying to observe the boy. His heart once again pounded loudly in his chest but this time it wasn't fear that was making it do it but some other emotion which he couldn't name.

The boy was fidgeting on the chair and doing something with his right hand to the neck of the instrument. He was going on and on and Franz couldn't figure out what was happening. But then the boy stopped, leaned back in the chair, raised his left hand with the bow, and froze still, his eyes closed as the night before, apparently getting ready to play.

Something strange then happened to Franz. He remembered the lump of coal he was carrying in his pocket and without knowing why he was doing it he stuck his hand in the pocket, got the lump out, stepped out from behind the pillar, and threw it at the boy, aiming at his head.

Like a fierce black bird it flew straight up until it was close to the boy and then swooped down steeply and dug itself into his right temple.

The boy sat still for a moment as if unaware of what had happened because of being engrossed in getting ready to play but then slowly leaned forward and fell onto his right side letting go of the bow but clutching the woman-violin as if afraid to go down alone. It rolled away from him however as if not wanting to have anything to do with him any longer and rested on the ground next to him after making a loud angry sound.

The lump of coal was nowhere to be seen but a black cat materialized from somewhere and scurried off scared, vanishing into thin air. It must have been sitting under the chair. A stream of blood then crept out from under the boy's head and like a thin red snake quickly slithered along the slabs with which the passageway was paved toward the black shadow cast by the arch. It seemed to want to get out of the sun as soon as possible.

Franz turned cold on seeing what had happened. The sides of his head along his temples were numb like wood and hair stirred on his head. What has he done?! He has killed the boy and now will be punished for it! They will probably put him to death! His only remedy was to flee.

He turned around and ran as fast as he could away from the scene of his crime. He started out along the passageway but then got out into the square thinking he was less likely to be seen there by someone coming out of the hotel door.

9. the funeral

• A wreath was forged out of iron consisting of vines, leaves, and blossoms and the sound of the hammer hitting the red-hot metal on the anvil echoed frightened in the empty smithy, escaping finally through the open door into the crisp morning air. In spite of it being summer there was frost on the plants.

• They carried the bed and the rest of the furniture out of the room, cleaned off the cobwebs in the corners and under the ceiling with a broom wrapped in a rag, and swept up the floor, all to reveal the room's true dimensions which turned out to be those of a perfect cube

• All watches and clocks were crushed like cockroaches on the floor.

• The canopy on the hearse was supported by four black posts with silver fluting chosen to resemble the bulging eyes and bared teeth of a vicious dog.

• What furniture and personal effects didn't fit onto the hearse were carried by the people walking in the procession behind it.

• They were all thrown pell-mell together with the coffin into the grave which had been dug big enough to contain them.

• Two skinny dogs appeared from nowhere in the middle of the ceremony and started devouring the earth piled up high in a cone next to one of the corners of the grave and two men, tall and thin, wearing black top hats, black stove-pipe pants and likewise black shoes with very pointed toes, chased them away by kicking them in the ribs. They were the only men in the crowd to wear such shoes and they wore the latter precisely for that purpose—to better chase the dogs away when they showed up. The earth was red and so were the dogs and the reason the dogs wanted to eat the earth was to maintain the color of their hair.

• What's for supper? His father asked in an angry voice abruptly turning away from the corner when he finally came home late that night.

• Franz wondered what would happen if you fried a watch like an egg.

10. franz leaves home

Franz was leaving home for good. He was dressed in black pants with tight legs which reached below his knees and a clean white shirt with sleeves too short to button and on his feet had high-topped brown shoes without laces made from leather grown hard from having been wet too often that looked like iron. He wore no socks and the shoes chafed his feet but they were hardened up enough by wearing so that they weren't about to blister or become raw. Franz wasn't even aware of the discomfort they caused him.

Over his right shoulder he held his favorite heavy stick on the end
of which hung a bundle made from his mother's checkered blue
and white kerchief which somehow escaped the purge, with a
change of clothing, a few personal items, a lump of bread, and a
big onion in it. In his left pocket he carried a bottle of water
sealed with a piece of rag tied into a wad.

The town of Blutburg lay about a quarter of a mile behind him
and he was moving in westerly direction with a slight southern
bend which is where he felt lay the land of blooming lemon trees,
oranges gleaming among dark leaves, still myrtle, tall laurel, and
so forth.

It was early morning and the sun had just come up, making
everything cast long shadows, all leaning in the direction he
walked. This included the rocks with which the earth was strewn
and even grains of sand, and of course him himself—his giant
shadow split at the bottom into a fork (his legs) reached almost to
the horizon. The earth curved so pronouncedly that he had
trouble walking and at times had to dig the sides of his shoes into
the hard soil so as not to slide back. The landscape was
completely bare and its sharp red arc on the horizon contrasted
sharply with the blue of the cloudless sky promising marvelous
unnamable things and events.

the quarry

"Es ist ein eigentümlicher Apparat," sagte der Offizier...

Franz Kafka

I. the quarry

Outside the town there is a quarry where a boy ten years old is being kept. Its walls go more than one hundred fifty feet up and are unscalable, being nearly vertical and perfectly smooth. The quarry is round and measures about a thousand feet in diameter. Its bottom is flat, strewn with boulders and overgrown with bushes and coarse sparse grass. A tiny brook dissects the quarry in two flowing out from a hole under one of its sides and disappearing in another one on the opposite end. It grows dry during prolonged periods of drought in the summer but during the rest of the year it flows full. The bottom of the quarry stays reasonably dry even during heavy rainfalls but in exceptionally wet years it floods to a height of as much as three feet. It takes then weeks to dry out.

There are holes in the sides of the walls here and there including and especially on the very bottom and the few deeper ones form what may be considered shallow caves.

The land around the edge of the quarry on top is flat and covered with thick short grass and bushes similar to the ones on the bottom.

A barbed wire fence runs around the perimeter of the quarry about one hundred feet from its edge so that it cannot be seen from the bottom, encircling it completely. There is a gate in the fence on the side of the quarry facing the town with a small wooden barrack next to it that serves as the command post. A sentry box stands next to it. A sentry is posted near the gate day and night marching back and forth with a long rifle that has a likewise long bayonet affixed to it on his shoulder. There are three more sentry boxes positioned at equal distances from each other along the outside of the fence with a sentry next to it carrying a similar rifle and marching day and night in similar fashion back and forth.

Stations are set up among the bushes inside the fence close to the edge of the quarry in such a way that they cannot be seen from the bottom that include high-powered telescopes on metal stands, fixed wooden tables and benches respectively to write and sit on, and telephones for the purpose of communicating between the stations as well as with the command post all for the purpose of spying on the boy and reporting on it. There are seven of these distributed at unequal distances from each other around the edge of the quarry in such a way that the boy can be seen from at least two of them at the same time no matter where he might find himself at a given instant in the open.

At night binoculars with infra-red capabilities are used to keep track of him if it is so desired.

2. a visit

Thin gray clouds above the quarry cover the sky like the short mustard-brown grass the ground below. The former is the same color as the uniforms of the sentries patrolling along the fence and the tarpaulins covering the objects in the spying stations.

Two boys approach the fence from the direction of the town walking along grass. They both look the same age—ten—except one of them is small for his years and the other one big—nearly a full head taller. The smaller boy has straight blond hair carefully combed and trimmed short, a smooth oval face with fine features, and blue eyes, and is dressed in a white short-sleeved shirt and short gray pants cut off almost at the groin. He wears white socks and good quality white sandals on his feet. The tall boy has very thick dark hair that has grown over his ears and onto the neck in the back and falls down over his forehead nearly hiding his deep-set dark eyes. It looks like a big fur hat fit for an adult rather than a boy. His face is long and bony with hollow cheeks and a long curving nose. He is dressed in a dirty long-sleeved white shirt somewhat small for him and with a button missing on the right sleeve and tight black shorts which reach below his knees. He wears badly worn heavy shoes the color of rusty iron on his likewise bare feet. The shoe strings on them have been broken in a few places and are tied in big careless knots.

The boys walk next to each other, the smaller one on the right of the bigger one, and stop about thirty feet away from the sentry.

The latter has been pacing back and forth about five steps on each side of the sentry box which is painted with red and mustard-brown diagonal stripes. On seeing the boys stop he stops himself, turns toward them, takes his rifle off his shoulder, aims it at the boys without pressing its butt to his shoulder, and opens and closes the lock on the gun without putting the bullet in the chamber, making a loud dry sound. He stares at them sternly without saying a word.

As that happens he boys quickly turn around and run down the slope in the direction they came from, the smaller one first and the bigger one following him, seemingly reluctant, as if being pulled by an invisible rope attached to his companion. They look like a couple of boulders rolling on their own, the smaller one first and the bigger one lazily behind it.

The town fills the broad flat valley nestling among the low rolling hills covered with the same kind of short mustard-brown grass as that around the quarry. There are no trees visible on any of them except here and there clusters of round bushes like those around the quarry.

The houses in the town for the most part have white walls and red-tiled roofs from among which here and there again stick up spires of churches, some sharp, Gothic- style, and others with round cupolas, Baroque. The crosses on them cannot be seen.

3. garbage

An observer and a visitor on a bench next to each other at one of the spying stations behind a bush. A telephone and a pair of binoculars on the table before them (before the observer). The telescope on its stand next to the table on the right (visitor's) side.

The visitor (in a hushed voice): So you dump the stuff every day... I mean night?

The observer (*amused, in a similar voice*): No, not every night... not even once a week.... Twice a month perhaps... or at the most three times.... But if there's a need we'll do it once a week... not sooner.

The visitor (*loudly*): You mean if there isn't enough food in the load?

The observer (*in a whisper; puts his index finger to his lips*): Shhh.... He mustn't hear us. (*Back to answering the question.*) That's right... If we see that there's nothing left for him to find we bring in a new load. (*Chortles.*) The good Lord always provides.... Don't we all feel that way until the day that he doesn't?

The visitor doesn't comment. Resumes his questioning after a pause.

The visitor (*likewise whispering; the conversation continues this way until when noted otherwise*): And you do this always at night?

The observer: Yes, when he's asleep, so that he doesn't see us.

The visitor: And he has never been woken up by the noise?

The observer: We don't think so although we don't know. But it doesn't matter in the end because he knows it's coming from the outside. So someone must be dumping it. But he mustn't see who's doing it....see even the outline of the people... so that he might think it's coming by itself... (*Through a half-smile.*) The good Lord always provides.... So we take special care. The personnel are dressed in black and wear black face masks.... And it's always at night.

The visitor (*still unbelieving*): And the noise of the engine doesn't wake him up?

The observer (*smiling*): Oh we don't bring it in a truck. We do bring it in from the town in a truck but then transfer it to a cart and pull it over by hand to the edge and dump it quietly and quickly... preferably in one dump.... There isn't much noise.... Just the stuff falling... But it's in the middle of the night when he's sound asleep.

The visitor (*still not quite satisfied*): And you dump it always in the same spot?

The observer: Pretty much so.... Roughly in the same area... as you saw. (*Points with his finger through the bush.*) Over there.... But we vary it a little so that the new stuff doesn't fall on top of what's left.... So that he has a chance to pick out everything... and so that everything decays quickly and doesn't fester... I mean rot... underneath.... We don't want any disease to start from there. (*After a pause.*) But we also don't want to mess up the whole area... to stink it up.... So we stick to that part of the quarry.

The questions that had arisen in the visitor's mind have been answered and he pauses to come up with new ones. This happens in a few seconds and he continues.

The visitor: That's food.... And he drinks from the brook?

The observer: That's right.

The visitor: And what about clothes? Does he get them from what's dumped too?

The observer: That's right.... Everything.... Food, things to make utensils with, bedding, clothes....

The visitor (*incredulous*): But is there enough stuff for him to clothe himself in?

The observer: There is.... Not that much but over a period of time... a few months... something always turns up.... At least it has so far. You'd be surprised how much useful stuff is being thrown away all the time even by people who don't have that much themselves.

The visitor (*still unbelieving*): And in the winter... he has enough clothes to keep himself warm?... When it gets really cold?

The observer: So far it hasn't been a problem. But we haven't had bad winters in the last few years.

The visitor: But what if it got really cold and he didn't have warm clothes? What would you do?

The observer: Oh we would then do something.... Make sure there're enough things in what we dump.... But as I said so far it hasn't been a problem and we didn't have to do it. (*After a pause.*) And I don't think we ever will.... Things always somehow work themselves out in the end.

The visitor (*pressing on*): And with food too?... If there weren't enough food in the stuff you bring in from the town you'd add something yourself?

The observer: In theory yes, of course.... We wouldn't let him starve to death. That's not the object. But so far we never had to do it and again I don't think we ever will. People always throw things out you can eat.... Even people that don't have much themselves as I said earlier.... We are a very wasteful society. (*After a pause.*) He'll always be fine.

The visitor (*quickly, as if afraid he will loose his train of thought*): And what if he got sick? Would you rescue him?... Bring him up or send down a doctor?

The observer (*grows serious; waits; then speaks in a normal voice*): The object is for him to survive on his own. His wits must be quick enough and his body strong enough for him to do it.

The visitor (*amazed and clearly upset but likewise in a normal voice*): So you mean you would let him die down there if he didn't get well on his own!

The observer (*a sign of confusion appears on his face; he quickly gets a hold of himself however and speaks again in a normal voice in a calm and measured way*): We believe it will never come to that. We believe that his body is strong enough and his mind tough enough for him to cope with anything that may come his way. Judging from what we know of him so far there will never be any need for us to intervene on his behalf. He will live to a ripe old age and will die of natural causes. We are sure of that.

It isn't certain if the observer has stopped for good or will continue. The visitor waits to find out. There are momentarily no questions in his mind and he waits. The silence continues like a drone.

4. sand

The boy's dream.

It is night. Everything is dark around him except the sky straight up is lighter—gray rather than black although there are no stars in it. He sits in his cave with his back to the wall, legs drawn up, his arms around them, waiting for the garbage to be thrown down. It has been days since the last dump and he is ravenous. Saliva is gathering in his mouth at the thought of eating and drips out of its corners onto his bare chest. It feels unpleasant and from time to time he wipes it off with his hands. This makes him think of a dog drooling and time and time again he tries to push the thought out of his mind but it just won't go away.

Suddenly he hears sounds coming from the opposite end of the quarry where garbage is usually dumped. They are soft and whooshing like the sound of water coming down. He jumps to his feet and sees big white stains coming down from above against the distant dark wall. They do look like water rushing down in a waterfall except not continually but in splashes. Higher up on the rim he sees the outlines of dark figures moving around furtively as they always do.

They are dumping garbage—and so soon! They have never done it so quickly after the previous dump. He is overjoyed, rushes out of the cave, and runs like mad through the dark space toward where the garbage is falling.

He can't see anything because of the darkness and runs into boulders, hurting his hands, knees, and forehead, gets entangled in bushes which clutch him with their sharp, scratchy, claw-like branches, stumbles on rocks, and sprawls on the ground face down hurting his hands and knees again, but always jumps up and keeps on running.

Soon he is near where the garbage is falling and sees it looming white up ahead. It keeps coming down from above continually now like water in a regular waterfall and he can't wait until he is there. He will let it spill over him.

Finally he is there and dives under the stuff that falls down. It spills over his head like water splashing around, making him laugh with joy. They had never dumped so much garbage before! He spreads his arms out wide, opens his hands, and catches something round in both of them. It is fruit—an apple and a plum. He closes his eyes, bends his head down, and feeling the things raining down on him bites first into the apple and then into the plum. They are juicy and delicious. He proceeds devouring them.

Then the garbage stops falling. He has finished eating the apple and the plum and is down on his knees searching with his hands in the garbage around him. There is a huge pile of it and it feels soft and bouncy. He will never be able to eat up all that is hiding in it. He digs his hands in deeper, finds two firm round forms, pulls them out, and bites first into one and then the other. They are a potato and a tomato. The former is raw but he likes the taste of it this time. Usually he doesn't. The tomato is also raw and tastes delicious as always. In a few seconds he has eaten them both and starts looking for something new. He does this for a while, finds all kinds of fruit and vegetables, eats them, and finally has had enough of them. He will look for something else. He digs his hands in deeper than ever before, almost up to his armpits, and comes across something soft and moist. He pulls it out and sees it is a huge piece of meat. He stands up and holds it out in his hands and it drapes from them like a piece of heavy blanket soaked in water. He will take it to his cave and eat it there.

He gets off the pile of garbage and runs again. This time for some reason his way stays clear for a while but then suddenly he catches his foot on something like a root and sprawls on the ground face down. He tries not to let the meat fall onto the ground but even though it stays in his hands it does this anyway and he is upset about it. He sits up and decides to eat the meat right there. He bites into it, tears off a big chunk, and starts chewing on it. It is covered with sand which crunches unpleasantly under his teeth but he disregards it and goes on chewing. He swallows the piece, tears off another one, and proceeds eating like that. The meat has no taste but he doesn't notice it as if this is the way it should be. Sand collects in his mouth as he goes on eating however and with time it builds up inside it. It fills the space between his gums and cheeks and gets all piled up in the back between his jaws so that he has trouble chewing. Then his mouth is full of it and he can't bite anything let alone chew. He starts choking on the sand and can't breathe. He will suffocate! In despair he tries to shout and wakes up.

It was quiet and dark all around but through the wide opening of the cave he could see the sky was much lighter than the walls of the quarry. Soon it would be dawn.

5. riding

The commandant's daughter's dream.

She is standing on the edge of the quarry looking down. She is holding a rope which hangs down into the quarry all the way to the bottom. The boy is standing next to where it coils on the ground. He is looking up as if not knowing what she wants him to do. She yells for him to grab the rope and climb up. He shakes his head yelling back he is afraid of falling down. The rope might slip out of her hands. She replies that she is strong and will not let go of the rope. He should climb.

The boy still shakes his head and says he is afraid.

If he climbs out she will give him something to eat, she yells. She will give him an apple.

Will she really? He asks.

She will, she repeats. She has an apple in her pocket and she takes it out and shows it to the boy.

This changes the boy's mind and he says he will climb out. He asks her to hold the rope tight.

She sticks the apple back in her pocket, grabs the rope with both hands, and steps back so that the rope drapes over the edge of the precipice. The boy has vanished from her sight but he does start climbing—the rope tautens up and she steps back even further to hold it tight.

She can feel the boy climb by the periodic tugs on the rope and soon she hears the sounds his feet are making on the wall and even his breathing. Then his head pops up from under the edge of the precipice, he climbs out, comes up to her, and goes down on his knees.

She takes the apple out of her pocket and offers it for the boy to bite. He does this, chews on the piece, swallows it, and bites on the apple again.

She likes feeding the boy like that. It makes her think of an animal—a dog or a cat.

There is less and less of the apple left as the boy bites into it and she feels his lips and tongue touch her fingers as he is biting around the core. This is even more pleasant. She had a baby goat do that to her once and it was wonderful. There is just the bare core left of the apple now and she throws it away and sticks her fingers inside the boy's mouth. He sucks on them like the kid goat did that one time. The sensation is wonderful.

Then the scene changes and now she is sitting on the boy's shoulders with her legs hanging down his chest and he is galloping through the field carrying her along. She hits him with her heels in the ribs from time to time to make him go faster.

He is going fast but she wants to go still faster. She hits him real hard with her heels but this doesn't help. She yells for him to go faster and starts pulling on his hair.

As this doesn't help she digs her fingernails into his face and twists his head. This sill doesn't help however. She decides then to go for his eyes. This will make him do what she wants!

He can't see where he is running however and in addition worries about his eyes, so he twists his head way to the side and falls down.

She comes down with him and sprawls on the ground. She gets up instantly however and finds herself with a piece of short thick rope in her hand. It is much thicker than the one she had the boy climb out on. The boy stays lying on the ground and she starts hitting him with the rope. It is heavy and she can feel and hear it hit him with a thump. He has curled up in the fetal position on his side with his knees pressed to his chest and his hands around his head. She keeps on hitting him and gradually gets more and more tired. She doesn't know how much longer she can go on but is determined not to give up.

6. the rat

The same observer and a different visitor at a different spying station looking down into the quarry between the branches of a bush carefully so as not to be seen—the former through binoculars and the latter through the telescope. They are observing the boy who has just pounced on a rat and is holding it in his right hand.

The visitor (*excited, loudly*): Did you see him jump?!

The observer (*concerned, softly*): Shhh.... He mustn't hear us. (*In a whisper. The conversation continues this way until noted otherwise.*) Yes, he has gotten to be pretty quick.

The boy is framed in the viewer of the telescope as if in a glass cage. He is tall and thin, with matted dark hair that falls below his shoulders and over his eyes. His face is black with grime and when he tosses his head to better see the whites of his eyes flash blinding white contrasting sharply with the dirty skin. His teeth are blinding white too and they flash like the blade of a knife catching sunlight when he opens his mouth. He wears a loose sleeveless garment of an indeterminable color (dark gray but this is probably only because of its being dirty) which reaches to below his knees and looks like a man's jacket with the sleeves torn off and holes in it all over through which you can see his body. It is naked and looks surprisingly clean, almost lily-white and therefore very delicate, unequal to the difficult task it is faced with.

The boy holds the rat high up by its back squeezing it tightly as it wriggles desperately in his grip. There is a satisfied sneer on his face.

Suddenly he grabs the rat's head with his left hand, brings the rat close to his mouth, adjusts the grip of his right hand, and bites the rat on its neck trying to sink his teeth in deep.

He shakes his head violently from side to side like a dog trying to kill an animal it has caught visibly straining in order to make his teeth go in deeper. This lasts a few seconds only however—five at the most—and then he lets go of the rat with his left hand and lifts it high up so as to have a better look at it.

It hangs limp in his fist, clearly dead, a big red gash in its gray neck like a piece of ragged red rag.

Apparently satisfied with the job he has done the boy brings the rat back to his mouth and tears away with his teeth at its flesh in the spot he has bitten into. He tears off a piece of the flesh, chews on it, spits something out (probably a piece of the furry skin), goes on chewing for a few seconds, swallows what he has in his mouth, and bites into the rat again. This time he tears off a big piece of the skin, spits it out, and tears away at the flesh he has cleared off.

The visitor (shocked): My God! He's a savage!

The observer doesn't react to what the visitor said as if not having heard him and keeps on looking attentively through the binoculars.

Down below the boy continues skinning the rat with his teeth and tearing away at its flesh.

The visitor is visibly upset at what he sees and leans away from the telescope.

The visitor (scrunching up his face, in disgust): Whew!

The observer (continues looking, casually): It's not a pleasant sight to be sure.

The visitor: Does he eat like this all the time?

The observer (*still looking*): No. It differs. Sometimes he eats quite normally, even daintily... surprisingly so. (*After a pause.*) He must be excited by the catch... and hungry.... We haven't thrown anything down to him for a while. (*He takes the binoculars away from his eyes and holds them in his hands on the table. Turns to the visitor and speaks in a normal but soft voice.*) He's really good with the rats... an excellent hunter.... Catches lots of them with his hands or kills them with a club or a stone. His aim is fantastic. He skins them and lets them dry in the sun to have when there's nothing else.... Impales them on sticks and sticks them in the ground... in long rows.... They look like crucifixions... offerings.... (*After a pause.*) He has a place for that... where there's lots of sun, facing south.... You can't see it from here. We'd have to move to another station. (*After a longer pause.*) Do you want to look at it?

The visitor (*likewise in a normal but soft voice, sincere*): Yes, of course. (*Almost immediately, clearly intrigued by the subject.*) You mentioned offerings.... Do you think those impaled rats are offerings?... To gods?... God?

The observer (*calmly*): I don't think so. He eats them so they couldn't be offerings. He doesn't seem to worship anything.

(Hesitates.)   But perhaps.... You never know.... *(Changes the subject. Getting up.)* Come let's go and have a look.

The visitor gets up.

7. the escape

For days the boy has been piling up garbage against the wall where it is always dumped and has built up a mound about fifteen feet tall. Then he has built something resembling a scaffold on top of the pile which goes up roughly another ten feet.

It is puzzling. What is he trying to do? Climb out? There is no way he can build some kind of a structure that would go all the way to the top—another hundred and twenty-five feet or so. And climbing up the sheer wall is impossible.

Still one morning he appears at the scaffold wearing a piece of cloth wrapped tightly around his loins and a tattered tight-fitting shirt with a bottle full of water and what appears to be a bundle of provisions tied to his back and starts climbing up the scaffold.

He must be planning to climb out of the quarry and envisions it to take him a long time.

How is he going to do it?

He reaches the top of the scaffold in a matter of seconds and surveys the wall above him. Then he starts climbing, finding little crevices in the rock into which he sticks his fingers and projections on which he steps with the sides of his feet or toes or grabs onto. He has been seen climbing up the wall like this before and it appears it wasn't just to amuse himself but to practice with his escape in mind.

But how is he going to make it all the way to the top? It is unthinkable that he has enough strength and stamina to climb that high without gloves and shoes even if there were enough irregularities in the rock for him to stand on and hold on to. He is plainly foolish.

But the telescope reveals there is a little niche not quite a foot deep and about three feet tall and wide about fifteen feet higher above the top of the scaffold and somewhat to the right. It is toward it that he is climbing. He will rest there and then climb on toward another niche if there is one.

And there is another niche about twenty or twenty-five feet higher directly above the first one. There are more similar niches and narrow ledges at roughly the same distance from each other what looks like to the very top of the wall in that spot. The boy must have done his homework! He must have studied the walls of the quarry carefully and selected the easiest path for him to climb along. And it happened to be where the garbage is being dumped which made it easier for him to stack it up and get a slight head start. By resting up in places where it is possible for him to do it and fortifying himself during those times with what he has brought along he might be able to get to the top of the wall even if it takes him a while! He certainly is very determined and clever. But given the circumstances he has been forced to live in he has to be. It was to be expected that if he were able to survive under the conditions in which he is being kept he should be the kind of person who would try to get out of the quarry if it were at all possible.

He is making slow but steady progress. His body clings to the wall as if held by suction and his hands and feet perform a complex slow-motion dance which makes him advance all the time higher and higher and at the same time to the right. Occasionally he takes a rest when he finds a good enough spot to do this, checks if he is moving in the right direction, and then climbs on.

About twenty minutes have gone by and he has reached the first niche, has climbed inside it, and is resting there, his feet on the ledge, his chest and left cheek pressed to the rock, his hands holding onto its edges. He breathes heavily and his face shows signs of exertion.

He rests for about five minutes and when his breathing has gotten normal he turns his head right and craning his neck looks downward to see how much he has climbed. He appears to be pleased with what he has accomplished and after waiting for about another five minutes sticks his head out of the niche and surveys the wall about him in preparation for climbing again.

He appears to have decided on his path and after searching with his hands for something to grab on to he moves out of the niche and resumes climbing.

The next niche as was said is another twenty or twenty-five feet almost directly above the first one. The boy climbs to the right however at about the same angle as he had climbed before either out of habit or because of not being sure where the second niche is. After he climbs some fifteen feet however he realizes he has made a mistake and tries to correct it. He looks for something to grab on to but there isn't anything. To move back to the left he will have to move down a few feet and then go straight up. He tries to move down but then his left foot slips, his fingers are unable to hold his weight, and he falls down along the surface of the wall. He doesn't seem to have made any sound while slipping (doesn't seem to have screamed) but he is probably too far away to be heard even if he did. (Being used to living alone he might have lost the instinct of calling out for help. So it is possible he hasn't bothered screaming.)

His light body moving on the dark background of the wall looks like a foamy patch in a waterfall spreading and contracting, changing its shape as it plummets faster and faster. It rotates clockwise as it falls and lands on its right side.

The boy has fallen beyond where he had piled up the garbage although there is still a little of it there. His body blends in with where it is piled up against the wall so that it is hard to find it. It can be made out in the end however. The bottle and the bundle of provisions are nowhere to be seen. They must have fallen off his back and landed somewhere else.

The boy lies still his face turned to the wall with no sign of life. He isn't stirring and his chest doesn't seem to move. Is he dead?

No, he isn't. After a few minutes he stirs. He has survived the fall.

He stirs a few more times and slowly rolls over onto his back. He must have hurt himself badly because his face is twisted with pain.

Sweat has run down it and left wide white marks on the grimy skin like traces of big fat worms. He takes short shallow breaths and keeps on grimacing from time to time as if the pain came in spurts.

Little by little he calms down however and starts raising himself on his arms. He props himself up on his left arm and reaches out with his right hand for his right leg. He raises himself some more on his left arm and puts his right hand on his right leg below his knee.

He falls back instantly however apparently having caused himself more pain. His face is twisted out of shape with pain. He must have injured his right leg badly—probably broken it.

He lies motionless for a while and then slowly rolls over onto his left side trying not to move his right leg. He rests in this position for a while, raises himself up on his left elbow, looks at his right leg, touches his right thigh with his right hand, apparently feels no extra pain, moves the hand down to the knee, massages the knee, again apparently does not feel any extra pain, then pulls the leg up a little with his hand, grimacing as he does that.

He lies back on his left side again, rests with his eyes closed breathing normally, then raises himself up on his left elbow again, and stares in the opposite direction to the other side of the quarry. It is where the cave he usually stays in is.

He waits a few seconds, twists his body in the direction he had looked in, and starts crawling forward. He pushes himself with his left arm and leg keeping the right leg dragging on the ground. From time to time it catches on something and then pain shatters his face like a rock breaking a mirror. He continues moving forward however. He moves slowly but makes continuous progress. From time to time he rests breathing heavily lying flat on the ground.

While crawling he stares with his eyes and mouth wide open in the direction he is moving an expression of infinite hope on his face as if certain help is awaiting him there which will put an end to his suffering.

8. shooting

The observer's dream.

He is looking at the boy down in the quarry through the telescope on his rifle. The perfectly formed thin black cross follows the latter continually dissecting his body into four equal quadrants.

It is summer. The sun is strong and the boy is naked except for the usual dirty white cloth tied around his loins. He is walking around in a bare spot among the bushes looking attentively at the ground before him. He seems to be looking for something or trying to find a spot well suited for whatever he wants to do.

His skinny back is bent into an arc and shines with sweat. The bumps on his spine run like a string of beads forced under his skin down the middle of his back from above his shoulder blades almost to his waist.

The boy must have found what he was looking for. He stops.

His finger is on the trigger, he squeezes it, hears the puff-like sound of the bullet coming out of the barrel muffled by the silencer, and sees the boy crumple down on the ground like a stiff cloth. He has hit him square between the shoulder blades where the bumps start. You can see the black hole where it has entered like a big fly that has settled there.

The boy lies still with his face down, his body in an awkward position, his long hair like a pot of black ink spilled in front of him.

It is possible the boy hasn't been killed because of where he has been hit so he centers the cross hairs on the boy's head, makes sure his own hands are steady, and squeezes the trigger.

The same sound is heard, the boy's body stirs like something light disturbed by a puff of wind, and stays still.

He can't see if he has hit the boy in the head because of the hair but he most probably has. There is no sign of a bullet hole on the body except for the first one and he couldn't have missed completely. He wants (has) to make sure though the boy is dead so he decides to fire again.

He aims at the boy's body almost at random somewhere around the middle of his back and fires.

The body jumps up like an item of clothing hit with a stick.

He has to be absolutely sure the boy is dead and fires again this time without much thought were he is aiming.

The body jumps up as the last time.

Then he stops planning and fires on and on purely at random.

He must be missing frequently now because dust rises up from the ground from time to time as he fires obscuring the body. Some of his shots obviously are hitting the body however because it jumps up now and then.

He is determined to go on firing forever but eventually when he squeezes the trigger nothing happens. He has emptied the magazine.

The dust has settled on the ground and he can see the boy's body spread out on it like a twisted up item of clothing. It lies still face down and he can see black holes all over the back and the side facing him. They look like flies that have come to feast on it.

There is nothing coming out of the holes but something dark is spreading on the ground around the boy's torso. It must be blood flowing out from where the bullets have come out underneath.

There is no doubt the boy is dead. He has accomplished his task.

9. mmmmm

The boy's dream.

It is night. The field stretches flat in all directions covered with tall silvery grass that reaches up to his knees and shimmers in the moonlight. The moon is full high up in the silvery sky.

He keeps on walking and the grass tickles his bare legs. There must be dew on it because his skin keeps on tickling even after he lifts his feet out of the grass.

Suddenly not far ahead trees appear like clouds of black fog rolling on the ground and from behind them shine through some yellow lights. There must be a house there.

He walks in among the trees and sees that a house does stand in fact a little farther among them. It has a tall dark roof and white walls. The latter shine bright in the moonlight.

The windows in the house are lit up with a soft warm light the color of honey. They are all open and an indescribably beautiful sound comes flowing out of them. It is a woman singing. He has never heard anything so beautiful in his life and feels he has to see who it is that sings.

He passes between the trees and the house is just a few steps before him.

There is a door in the center of its front wall and it is dark and closed.

It doesn't matter. He will open it and go inside.

He comes up to the door, puts his hand on the handle, pushed down on it, and the door opens obediently, letting him in. He is now inside the house.

It is totally filled with the soft honey light which blinds him so that he can't see anything. But the woman keeps on singing.

Then suddenly she is in front of him. Her face is framed in long hair the color of dark honey and radiates kindness and warmth. A pair of huge blue eyes stare at him smiling. She has been waiting for him! His eyes fill with tears. He tries to say something in return but his lips won't open as if permanently stuck together trying to make the sound "mmmmm."

10. flood

It is cold. Thick dark clouds hang low over the land. It is not raining but the ground is soggy with water which has gathered here and there along it in shallow pools. It must be the rainy season and therefore likely it will rain again soon.

The four sentries march back and forth in front of their boxes like pendulums swinging first this way then that about their points of suspension. Their steps are even like the ticking of a clock. Although moving constantly the bayonets on the end of the rifles seem stuck painfully into the sky like needles deep into a person's flesh.

Down below in the quarry all is still. Water has filled its bottom to what looks like the depth of a foot hiding under it the grass and most of the debris leaving only boulders and bigger bushes to stick out. They are reflected in its surface as if in a mirror adding a touch of beauty to the bleak scene. When an occasional gust of wind makes its way to the bottom of the quarry it causes the water to ripple in big dark burrs.

Over where garbage is dumped some of it has risen to the surface and floats in the water lifeless like drowned persons lying face down with their limbs floating alongside them,

There is no sign of life anywhere.

II. a game

The sunshine presses down on the earth like a huge stone slab on a person's shoulders certain to crush eventually him or her. It is stifling hot up above in the open but must be unbearable in the quarry below.

The boy has been doing something with his hands squatting down on the ground and then gets up and goes into the cave swaying from side to side as he limps on his crooked right leg. After a few seconds he comes back. It isn't clear why he had gone into the cave since it doesn't seem that he took anything with him or has brought anything back.

He sits down on the ground in the spot he had squatted in before with his legs crossed, leaning forward, his head hanging down. He is naked except for a piece of dirty white cloth tied around his loins.

He has grown even thinner than he has been lately.

His spine stands out sharp under his skin almost about to tear through in places, his ribs seem two huge hands with many fingers greedily clutching his torso from below, and when he moves one of his arms its shoulder blade looks like the wing of a giant insect rearranging itself so as to find a more comfortable place to rest in. It seems to permanently reside there. The two tendons on the sides in the back of his head look like pegs that have been stuck under his skin to help support it. It seems it is too big and heavy to stay up by itself.

He has cut his hair short apparently with something sharp like the top of a tin can or a piece of glass—for obvious reasons very unevenly, sometimes right at the skin, at others much longer, perhaps as long as an inch. It covers his head like a ragged thatch.

Surprisingly his hair is light now, almost blond, probably partly because it is easier for him to wash it due to its being short and partly because it is bleached by the sun.

From what you can see of his face it looks clean. He seems to be washing himself at least sometimes. His body is tanned the color of polished bronze and shines with sweat.

The latter runs down his back and the side of his face in big drops. He seems to be oblivious of it however as he is bending down, pulling something out of the ground and then sticking it back in elsewhere.

What is he doing? Weeding? Pulling up sprouts and replanting them?

No, that couldn't be it. Those are little sticks which are dry and he is merely moving them around.

Is he preparing them to support plants which will grow along them?

That isn't it either. They are too short for that and too close together. Besides, they aren't smooth but shaped like little human figures with arms and sometimes legs, fashioned out of twigs.

It is odd.... They are arranged in two bunched up groups which face each other like armies in a field before a battle.

It doesn't make sense.... What in God's name is going on?

The observer (it is the same one again) picks up the telephone receiver, dials a single digit number on the telephone, and speaks into the mouthpiece. (He is calling a colleague at a different spying station.)

The observer (*in a hushed voice here and throughout the conversation*): What is he doing? I can't see him well from here. Can you? (*After a pause.*) I thought he was planting something but that's not it.

Voice in the receiver (*likewise hushed here and throughout*): No, he's not planting anything. That's what I thought too at first but it's not that. He seems to be playing a game.

The observer (*surprised, almost peeved*): A game? What sort of a game?... (*After a pause, incredulous.*) Chess?

Voice in the receiver (*hesitates*): I don't know.... (*Hesitates some more*). It could be chess.... There are two groups facing each other and there are bigger and smaller sticks... like pawns and other pieces.... And one or two on each side are bigger than the rest... like king and queen.... (*After a longer pause.*) But there are more than two rows on each side and they're too close together... too close to each other.... And there are way too many pieces.

The observer (*intrigued*): He might be trying to recreate what he remembers of the game of chess from his childhood.... He's too young to remember the rules if he ever played chess.... He may have just watched adults play and is sort of aping it now like kids do.

Voice in the receiver (*after some hesitation*): That could be it. (*After a long pause.*) But no, I doubt that. He just had one of the sticks... pieces... sort of grapple with the other one and then knock it over. Did you see it?

The observer (*regretful*): No, I couldn't from here. (*Excited.*) But that's it.... He probably thinks that that's what playing chess is.... Pieces fighting with each other and one knocking the other one down.

Voice in the receiver (*after a pause, excited*): No, no!... He has moved the two groups together... intermingled them.... Can you see it?

The observer (*also excited*): Yes... a little. (*After a pause.*) I don't understand what he's doing.

Voice in the receiver (*more excited*): They're in a battle... a fray.... Those are two armies fighting.... He's playing at soldiers fighting on a battle field.

The observer (*after a brief pause, likewise excited and amazed*): You're right! It's amazing he'd be playing a game like that!.... (*After a long pause.*) They're mowing each other down.

Voice in the receiver (*laughing*): His side is winning.... There are fewer and fewer of the other ones left.... Soon they'll be all gone.... He's going to win.... (*After a long pause, with contempt.*) Oh it's just a silly child's game. It's nothing.

sunday morning

I. church bells

From the valley behind them, from among the red-tiled roofs of homes and the dark green crowns of trees billowing around them, coming from one or perhaps more than one of the church spires sticking up sharply above the houses all over the town, they could hear the church bells ringing, calling people to mass. It was Sunday morning and they were walking along a dirt road on the crest of a hill outside the town, the strong sunlight beating down upon them, making them look sharp like a huge magnifying glass held above their heads. In the distance the dark mountains seemed giant whales frolicking in the sea, jumping out of the water and plunging gracefully back into it again. It was summer and the fresh air smelled of warmth.

We're not going to mass today, the boy said as if to himself but actually in order to hear his father's voice. He wore a short-sleeved white shirt open at the neck, short gray pants cut off almost at the groin, held up by suspenders of the same material, white socks neatly folded down over his ankles, and also white sandals cut out in an intricate pattern. His father was dressed in a white long-sleeved shirt open at the neck, a likewise gray suit with wide pants, and shiny black shoes. The pants swayed gracefully as he walked, their folds a visual accompaniment to his movement like delicate music. His jacket was draped loose over his shoulders and open up front. He had taken it off as they were climbing up the hill because he was getting hot. It was cooler on top but still too warm for him to put it back on properly.

You wanted to go for a hike in the country, so we will have to miss it today, his father answered. Unless you would like to go in the evening to vespers.

Yes, the boy said after thinking for a few seconds. I think we should... to pray for mommy to come back soon. Norma is praying for her now in church but we should do too, he concluded.

2. mother

Mommy will be back soon, right? He continued after a short pause. She just went to drink water to get better.

Yes, his father answered calmly. She won't be long. Just a few weeks or a month at the most and then she'll be back.

It will still be summer then, right? The boy asked anxiously. And warm.

Yes, his father said. It will be just like now.

And we'll all go swimming in the big river like we did last summer, the boy went on.

Yes, his father said. Just as we used to.

And mommy will prepare a picnic like she did last year, the boy said. This year when we went she didn't prepare one.

No she didn't because she wasn't feeling well, his father said. But when she comes back she will be feeling better and she will prepare a wonderful picnic like she always did, with cold meat, and pâté, and fresh bread, and salad, and fruit tart for desert, and lemonade to drink.

In the bottles you can close, the boy interrupted. I love those bottles. They're like big clear bubbles and have those white porcelain stoppers and the red rubber rings that go around them and they close real tight so that you can turn them upside down and they don't spill.

Yes, his father said. In bottles from seltzer water. And we will bring seltzer water too.

Yes, the boy said. I love seltzer water and the bottles it comes in... and the lemonade mommy puts in them. And Norma will come with us, he added as an afterthought.

Yes of course, she will, his father said. She always does. We're a family.

We're a family, the boy said softly to himself.

3. little nora

He looked straight up as he said that and added, But not little Nora.

No, his father said. Not little Nora.

She's up there, the boy said, pointing with his finger sharply into the sky like one of the church spires back in town.

Yes, his father said. In heaven.

With the angels, the boy said continuing as if not hearing his father.

Yes, his father said. With the angels.

A lark had been singing all along as they walked but the boy seemed to have noticed it only then. He saw the little dark shape tremble high above the earth as if from the effort of singing, imparting the shaking of its body to the sounds it was making.

Up there where the lark is? The boy asked not taking his eyes off the bird.

No, his father answered. Much, much higher. Way, way up.... Far away.... You can't see all the way there from here.

And she's waiting for us there? The boy asked, still looking up.

One day all of us will go there, his father said. And we'll all be there together as a family.

And we'll have picnics up there... as by the river... the five of us, the boy said.

No, his father said. You don't have picnics in heaven. You sing hymns there to God.

With the angels? The boy asked.

Yes, with the angels, his father answered.

Like the lark? The boy asked. He had finally lowered his head.

Even more beautifully than the lark, his father said.

Much, much more beautifully, the boy said again to himself.

Like the angels, the boy said softly once more to himself and then went on, And God made the lark by throwing it up into the sky.

No, his father said. Not the lark.... A lump of earth. And it turned into a lark and began singing.

Praising its maker for making it? The boy asked.

Yes, his father said. Praising God. Thanking him for making it a lark.

Like this? The boy said after bending down, picking up a lump of clay, and tossing it up with both hands. It flew only a few feet up however and fell down in front of them.

Yes, his father said. Except much, much higher.

Much, much higher, the boy said softly to himself again and then added louder, Because God is very strong.

Yes, his father said. God is very strong and he can do anything.

And he could make little Nora come back to us if he wanted to? The boy asked.

Yes, he could, his father said. But it wouldn't be right. She was destined to go to heaven when she was born and she must stay there.

To sing with the angels? The boy asked.

Yes, to sing praise to God with the angels, his father answered.

For making her go to heaven? The boy asked.

For creating her, his father said after hesitating for a while. And for letting her go to heaven.

And if mommy went to heaven, then God could make her come back to us, to be together as a family? The boy asked.

Yes, his father said, He could. But mommy isn't going to heaven now, so he won't have to do it. She'll be back soon and we'll go to picnics together by the big river.

Very soon? The boy asked.

Yes, his father said, Very soon. In a few weeks or a month at the most, and then everything will be as before.

As before, the boy said to himself and added barely audibly, And we'll be a family.

4. father

And you won't go away either? The boy asked after a while.

No, I won't, his father said.

Not even if they call you? The boy asked.

If they call me I would have to go, his father said after a brief pause. But they won't. Not right now. Maybe later... in the winter.... But I'd come back then... from time to time...often... and then for good, and everything would be as before.

And we'd be a family, the boy said, as if filling in for his father.

That's right, his father said. We'd be a family again, as always.

As always, the boy said, echoing his father's words.

But mommy would be home if you would have to go, the boy said with a trace of worry in his voice after a brief pause.

Yes, definitely, his father said firmly. Mommy would be home to stay with you and Norma if I had to go away.

And you would come back often and then for good? The boy asked.

That's right, his father said. At first often and then for good.

The boy had been walking a few steps ahead of his father on the left. He slowed down to let the latter catch up with him and raised his right hand to put it in his father's. The hands found each other and clasped together like two halves of a whole. The boy continued walking happily skipping along, clutching firmly his father's hand.

5. hand

There was grass growing on both sides of the road until then. A field of wheat now appeared on the right, with the grain in it not quite fully grown yet, about two feet high, and pale green in color, the beard on the end of the ears even paler like its shadow cast onto clear water.

The boy noticed it, freed his hand from his father's, ran up to the side of the field, grabbed a few of the ears in his hand, squeezed them tight, and held them for a few seconds.

He let go of them soon, ran back to his father, took his hand into his again, and said, No, it's not warm like your hand.

What? His father said, laughing. The ears of wheat aren't warm like my hand? Did you expect them to be?

No, the boy said. But they look beautiful, so I wondered if they were as warm as your hand, but they aren't. And I'm glad they aren't, he added after a while.

Why? His father asked, a trace of a smile still in his voice.

Because..., the boy hesitated, clearly not sure what to say, but then went on, Because I wouldn't like your hand so much if wheat could be as warm as it.... Because it wouldn't be so special.

I like your hand, he added after a while and quickly kissed it without letting go of it as they walked.

His father raised his left hand with that of the boy, bent down, kissed the latter,
and said, I like yours too.

The boy looked up at his father, smiled satisfied, and they walked on.

6. numbers

How much is two plus two? Asked the boy suddenly.

Four, his father replied quickly.

And two plus three? The boy went on.

Six, his father answered after a brief pause.

No, the boy laughed. It's five.

And five plus five? He went on.

His father hesitated a little longer and then said, Fifteen.

No, the boy laughed loudly. It's ten.

It's ten, you're right, his father agreed and then asked, And how much is four plus five?

Nine, the boy answered quickly.

And fourteen plus fifteen? his father continued.

The boy thought for a while and then said, Twenty-nine.

Correct, his father replied. And seventeen plus eighteen?

Thirty-four, the boy answered after thinking a little, but then corrected himself quickly, No, thirty-five. Seventeen plus ten is twenty-seven, and twenty-seven plus eight is thirty-five.

You're a smart little boy, his father said, stroking the boy's head with his right hand.

I like numbers, the boy said.

I know you do, his father said and then asked, Why do you like them?

Because they're clear, the boy replied after thinking for a while. Like water.... Like they are written on white paper in the water and you see them clearly and that's all. And they'll always be like that and nothing will hurt them.

You're right, his father agreed. Numbers will always be the way they are and nothing will ever change them.

They proceeded walking in silence, the boy skipping a few steps from time to time.

7. whales

Look, they're like whales, he suddenly said, pointing ahead with his left hand.

What is? His father asked, not understanding.

The mountains, the boy answered. They're like big whales jumping out of the water and going down again. Like in the book you gave me.

That's right, his father readily agreed. They're like a bunch of whales playing in the sea.

A school, the boy corrected him.

Yes, a school, his father said. A group of whales or other fishes is called a school.

Whales aren't fishes, the boy corrected his father. They're mammals. They have lungs. But fishes also swim in schools.

You're absolutely right, his father said, stroking the boy's head again. Whales aren't fishes but mammals, and both whales and fishes swim in schools.

They swallow men, the boy said after a while.

Jonah, his father said. He was swallowed by a whale.

And other men too? The boy asked.

Not normally, his father answered. They don't eat men.

They eat little fishes, the boy said. But they can swallow men and then spit them out alive.

They can do that, his father agreed. That's true.

And it's dark inside a whale's belly, right? The boy asked.

Yes, it pitch-black in there, his father said.

There're no holes there, the boy went on.

No, there're no holes, his father said.

And you can't look out the whale's eyes either, the boy said.

No, you can't, his father said, Because the eyes aren't in the belly.

That's right, the boy said. The eyes aren't connected to the belly.

The topic had been exhausted once more and the boy's thoughts drifted back to what they had talked about earlier.

8. norma

Will Norma play the piano when she's up in heaven with us? He asked.

I don't think there're pianos in heaven, his father answered.

Because they're too heavy? Because they'd fall down? The boy said quickly.

His father hesitated for an instant.

Partly because of that, yes, he said finally.

And because they play harps in heaven? The boy asked again quickly. Like the angels?

Yes, his father answered through a smile that had formed itself on his lips, Like the angels.

So Norma will play a harp with the angels? The boy asked.

Yes, his father answered after hesitating for a while, She will play the harp.

And we too? Are we all going to play harps? The boy asked.

His father hesitated a little longer this time. No, he said finally, We won't play harps. We will just sing... hum along.

To praise God? The boy asked.

Yes, to praise God, his father answered.

For making us? The boy asked.

Yes, for making us, his father answered patiently.

And for letting us come to heaven? The boy continued.

That's right, his father answered. For permitting us to enter his kingdom.

And because we don't know how to play? The boy continued.

Yes, his father answered. Because not all of us are musicians.

And Norma will play Krieg and Showpain? The boy pressed on. Together with the angels?

Grieg and Chopin perhaps, his father said. But also other music. The kind of music they play in heaven to praise God.

The boy had freed his hand from that of his father during the last stretch of the conversation and walked now alone with his head bent down, thinking.

9. chess

But God doesn't play the harp together with the angels and musician people who are in heaven, right? He said after a while.

No, he doesn't, his father replied. It wouldn't make sense. God wouldn't be praising himself.

It's not right to praise yourself, the boy said. And besides God is not his own maker.

Of course he's not, his father said. You can't make yourself.

Because you wouldn't be there to make yourself, the boy went on, reasoning.

You're absolutely right, his father said again putting his left hand on the boy's head and stroking it gently. And nobody made God, he added after a brief pause. He has always existed.

He has always existed, the boy said, once again echoing his father.

But God knows how to play the harp and could play it if he wanted to, he said after a few seconds' pause, returning to the previous subject.

Yes, he could, his father said.

And he knows how to play chess too, the boy said after another brief stretch of silence.

Of course he does, his father said. God knows how to do everything.

Does he play chess with himself sometimes like you do? The boy asked inquisitively.

Well..., his father hesitated briefly. He probably does sometimes. But he plays the world as if it were a big chess game. The atoms, and molecules, and planets, and stars I told you about, and everything else is like chess pieces and God plays with them as in an enormous chess game.

Moving them around? The boy asked.

Yes, sort of moving them around, his father answered.

And clouds in the sky too? The boy asked looking up.

Yes, and clouds in the sky also, his father replied.

So that's why they move? The boy asked.

Yes, his father answered. God moves them in the sky like pieces on a chess board.

And he has taken them all now, so that's why there aren't any? The boy continued.

Yes, his father said. He took them away as pieces off a chess board.

And little Nora too? The boy persisted. He took her like a pawn off a chess board.

Well, his father said hesitating once again. Not quite in the same way.... The world is a much more complicated game than chess.... God took little Nora to himself because she was destined to go to heaven when she was born.

To sing praise to him together with the angels for making her? The boy asked, returning to what they had talked about earlier.

That's right, his father said. To sing praise to her maker with the angels.

The boy remained silent, his questions answered for the time being. He continued thinking as he walked however.

10. rat

They were walking past a cabbage field on their left.

Did God create hares too? The boy asked. The hare that raced the hedgehog and lost?

Of course he did, his father said. God created everything.

And Mr. Hedgehog who won the race? The boy asked ignoring his father's answer.

As well as Mr. Hedgehog, his father answered calmly.

And Mrs. Hedgehog who helped him win the race? The boy went on.

Yes, and Mrs. Hedgehog also, his father said.

And rats too? The boy went on without a pause.

And rats too, his father answered patiently.

And he stuck a lump of earth in the hole in a wall for them to live in there? He asked.

Well, his father hesitated for an instant, He didn't necessarily stick it into a hole in a wall, but he took a lump of earth and made a rat out of it... told it to be rat.

But not the rat in the wall in our house, the boy said, Because it's not a rat but a boy.

Oh, that rat, his father said. I told you it's not a rat but a mouse. Rats don't live inside walls. They're too big. It's a mouse.

No, it isn't, the boy said emphatically. It's a rat. It couldn't be a mouse because a mouse is timid and the boy isn't and a rat isn't either. It's fierce. And it's big. I saw it. Like this.... (He held his hands about a foot apart.) And it turns into a boy when it comes out of the hole and back into a rat again to get back in. But the rat eats first before turning into a boy so as to have to eat less... the crumbs in the kitchen. For otherwise he'd be hungry. But then the rat turns into a boy for a while to thaw out.

To thaw out? His father asked, not understanding.

Yes, too thaw out from being a rat, the boy explained. And from being all cramped up inside the wall.... And once he thaws out he turns into a rat again and crawls back into the hole.

You've seen him? His father asked with interest. When?

Last week, the boy answered.

When? His father asked with more interest.

In the middle of the night, the boy said. When I got up to go to the bathroom. I went into the kitchen to see if the rat was there, and it was, and then all of sudden it was a boy, and he stood there looking at me.

What did he look like? His father asked.

Tall and skinny... with black hair, the boy said.

Not like you? His father continued.

No, not like me, the boy answered firmly.

Did he say anything? His father asked.

No, the boy said, He didn't say anything. He doesn't speak our language. He's not from here.

Oh, his father said. Where is he from?

Far away, the boy answered. From a foreign land. He lost his home and family, and he ran away as far as possible, and found our house, and lives here now.

Why does he stay inside the wall? His father asked. Why doesn't he come out?

He's afraid, the boy answered. He doesn't want anyone to see him.

Why? His father asked. Why is he afraid to be seen?

He's afraid they'll hurt him, the boy answered. People will hurt him.

Why does he think that? His father asked,

Because he's been hurt before, the boy said. And he thinks they'll hurt him again.

But he's not afraid of you? His father asked.

Not very much, the boy answered. Just a little. He still doesn't know me. But once he does know me he won't be afraid. We'll become friends.

Oh, his father said. And how will you communicate? What language will you speak to each other?

He will learn ours and I will learn his, the boy answered. And we'll use sign language at first. You don't have to speak to be friends, he added. You can just show.

I know, his father said. You don't need to speak to be friends.

And will you go to stay inside the wall with him? His father asked.

I don't know, the boy answered after some hesitation, obviously stumped by the question. I couldn't fit into the hole and inside the wall. I'd have to learn how to turn into a rat first. And I don't know how to do it.

Maybe he could teach me, he said after a while. But I'd rather not be a rat. I wouldn't want to live in a wall. It'd be dark there like inside a whale's belly. I wouldn't like it.

He seemed to want to drop the subject and took off running leaving his father behind.

II. sky

He stopped about a dozen yards ahead, turned around, and shouted to his father, Unless mommy, and you, and Norma were gone, and our house was empty.

He threw his head back and looked at the sky.

I know why he's afraid to come out too, he shouted. Because he doesn't want to fall into the sky and disappear in it. It's all empty

Yes, his father said quietly, nearing him. Everyone is afraid of that. It's lonely up there.

The lark could no longer be heard singing and was nowhere to be seen in the sky. The boy bent down, picked up a rock, and threw it as hard as he could skyward. It flew much higher than the lump of clay before but eventually fell down by the side of the road close by. The boy wanted to do this again with another rock but saw his father shaking his finger at him telling him not to do it. He knew it wasn't because he had used a rock instead of a lump of clay but because people shouldn't try making a lark out of a piece of dead matter. Only God could do it.

He stood patiently waiting for his father to come up but felt the latter was moving too slowly.

Come on dad, hurry up! He yelled. Let's get going!

synopsis

The themes of alienation, abandonment, and fear of death, developed in *Like Blood in Water*, the first book of *The Placebo Effect Trilogy*, are picked up in the second book, *The Future of Giraffes*, which is devoted to the topic of childhood. A boy takes a nap during a family picnic and finds himself all alone on waking up. A cognitively impaired savant boy decides he has had enough of living and trudges off to his grave. A boy leaves his hometown called Blood City in search of one like Menton after his mother's funeral. Another boy is kept imprisoned in a quarry in a barbarous experiment of survival. Still another one dreams of turning into a rat to hide in a wall so as not to be hurt by people when his parents are gone.

The five mininovels that make up *The Future of Giraffes*, as is the case with its two companions, all employ *negative text*—gaps of vital information which the reader is obliged to supply himself. By bringing personal experience into the story, the reader makes it more vivid and real, becoming in the process its co-author together with the author of the text.

biography

Yuriy Tarnawsky has authored more than two dozen books of poetry, fiction, drama, essays, and translations. He was born in Ukraine but raised and educated in the West. An engineer and linguist by training, he has worked as a computer scientist at IBM Corporation and professor of Ukrainian literature and culture at Columbia University. He writes in Ukrainian and English and resides in the New York City area.

His other English-language books include the books of fiction *Meningitis, Three Blondes and Death, Like Blood in Water* (all FC2), *Short Tails*, and *View of Delft* (both JEF Books), as well as the play *Not Medea* (JEF).

Great Works of Innovative Fiction Published by JEF Books

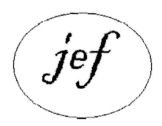

For a complete listing of all our titles
please visit us at experimentalfiction.com

CPSIA information can be obtained at www.ICGtesting.com
Printed in the USA
LVOW10s0045121114

413137LV00024B/877/P